POPULAR PUBLICATIONS   FACSIMILE EDITIONS

Shock #1
(March 1948)

Shock was launched in 1948 by Popular Publications as a companion magazine to its primary detective pulps, *Dime Detective* and *Black Mask*, concentrating on weird-mystery stories. The first issue contains stories by Frederick C. Davis, John D. MacDonald, Robert Turner, D.L. Champion, and Bruno Fischer.

Authors:

Frederick C. Davis, John E. Harbaugh, John D. MacDonald, H.C. Malcolm, Robert Turner, D.L. Champion, John Bender, Curt Hamlin, Jack Bennett, Bruno Fischer

Illustrators:

Frederick Blakeslee, Everett Raymond Kinstler, Monroe Eisenberg

BILL FOUND MORE THAN TREASURE WHEN...

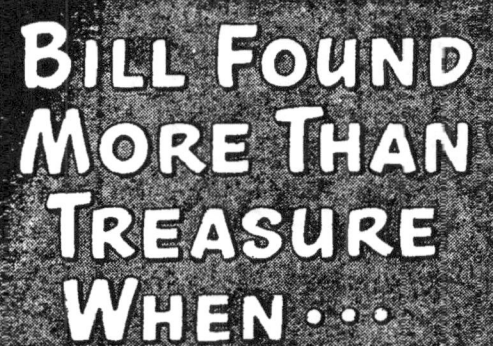

RADIO FROM THE "OLD MAN" HIMSELF. HE WANTS THIS CREW SENT TO HIS YACHT PRONTO!

WONDER WHAT'S UP?

CHIEF DIVER BILL ROBB, EX-NAVY SALVAGE OFFICER, IS RESTING BETWEEN DIVES TO A SUNKEN SHIP IN HOLLISTER BAY WHEN...

I HATE TO ASK THIS, ROBB, BUT MY NIECE LOST HER PURSE AND SOME VALUABLE JEWELRY OVERBOARD

I'LL HAVE A GO AT IT, MR. BAKER

WHAT LUCK! I'VE FOUND IT

NICE WORK, ROBB. COME ABOARD, I'D LIKE TO TALK OVER THAT "AURORA" JOB WITH YOU

AND ME WITH TWO DAYS' WHISKERS

I'LL DELAY INTRODUCTIONS UNTIL WE GET ROBB OUT OF HIS WORKING CLOTHES

WHAT A GIRL!

HERE'S SHAVING TACKLE AND SOME CLEAN WHITES

THANK YOU, SIR

WHAT A SLICK-SHAVING BLADE! SOMETHING SPECIAL, SIR?

WELL, YOU COULD SAY SO... THIN GILLETTES ARE EXTRA KEEN AND LONG-LASTING

I HANDLED A SIMILAR SALVAGE JOB IN NAPLES AND IT WORKED PERFECTLY

H-M-M, THINK YOU COULD HANDLE THIS ONE?

HE'S THE BEST-LOOKING MAN I EVER SAW

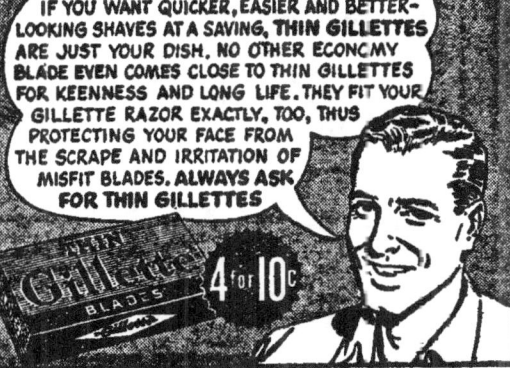

IF YOU WANT QUICKER, EASIER AND BETTER-LOOKING SHAVES AT A SAVING, THIN GILLETTES ARE JUST YOUR DISH. NO OTHER ECONOMY BLADE EVEN COMES CLOSE TO THIN GILLETTES FOR KEENNESS AND LONG LIFE. THEY FIT YOUR GILLETTE RAZOR EXACTLY, TOO, THUS PROTECTING YOUR FACE FROM THE SCRAPE AND IRRITATION OF MISFIT BLADES. ALWAYS ASK FOR THIN GILLETTES

GILLETTE BLADES 4 for 10¢

15¢

THE NEW MYSTERY MAGAZINE

SHOCK

Volume 1　　　　**March, 1948**　　　　**Number 1**

The next issue will be out March 19th.

Published bi-monthly by New Publications, Inc., at 2256 Grove Street, Chicago, 16, Illinois. Editorial and Executive Offices, 210 East 43rd Street, New York, 17, N. Y. Entry as Second-class matter pending at the Post Office, at Chicago, Illinois, under the Act of March 3, 1879. Copyright, 1948, by New Publications, Inc. This issue is published simultaneously in the Dominion of Canada. Copyright under the International Copyright Convention and Pan American Copyright Conventions. All rights reserved, including the right of reproduction, in whole or in part, in any form. Single copy, 15c. Annual subscription for U.S.A., its possessions and Canada, $.90; other countries 25c additional. Send subscriptions to 210 East 43rd Street, New York, 17, N. Y. For advertising rates, address Sam J. Perry, 210 East 43rd Street, New York 17, N. Y. When submitting manuscripts, enclose stamped, self-addressed envelope for their return, if found unavailable. The publishers will exercise care in the handling of unsolicited manuscripts, but assume no responsibility for their return. Any resemblance between any character, appearing in fictional matter, and any person, living or dead, is entirely coincidental and unintentional. Printed in the U.S.A.

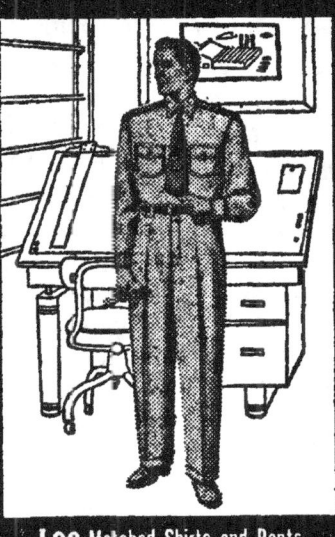 

Without Warning

THE room wasn't built for walking. Square and plain, with drab plaster walls, draperies fresh from the showroom of your cheap local dealer in furniture who makes your home look like "the home of the movie stars."

And yet she walked. Ceaselessly. From the bed to the bathroom door. Back. The wide windows looked down on the heart of the city. She felt the deep pulse of the city and it was something that was part of the beat of her heart, something that took possession of nerve, vein, reiterant pulse. . . .

There would be no point in calling the desk.

As soon as Karl came back from the meeting he would come to the room. There was nothing else he *could* do. It was his room. Karl was a creature of habit.

She paused, near the windows, held both hands outstretched, fingers spread, felt the excited surge of pulse that made her hands tremble, made a vein throb in her throat, made her feel once again the deep fear that had been with her ever since she had walked up the gangplank at Colombo.

On impulse, she hurried to the bureau, pulled open the drawers, ruffling impatiently through the neatly folded underthings, the starched shirts. It was in the second drawer. A plain silver flask bearing the odd seal she had learned to recognize. Just a plain silver flask, dull finish, inscribed with a warning that she could interpret.

She unscrewed the cork, tilted it high, and the sharp sting of the liquor tore at her throat. Of course it was good and expensive liquor. Karl would insist on nothing less. The deep rich glow warmed the chill of fear, made her strong again . . . and bold.

It was at that instant that she heard his key in the door. The knob turned. She stood, his silver flask in her hand.

He was startled at the glow of light in the room. She saw him blink against the glare, pause, iron out the expression of dismay.

His tone was most casual. "Hello, Stella." As though finding a woman in his room was a customary thing.

She heard, in her own voice, the thin fragile note of hysteria. "Karl!" she said. "How nice! Welcome home."

Without taking his eyes from her, he closed the door behind him. The click of the brass latch was thin, metallic, final, somehow ominous. Karl had become a quiet monster. Without warning. Without plan.

He walked toward her, stopped three feet away and said, "It is nice, isn't it?" His blue eyes were cold. "I saw Roger this evening. He told me—just enough."

Stella backed away suddenly as he reached for her. She couldn't evade the angry hand that reached for her throat, but tore the fabric of her dress.

Holding the dark green dress together, she backed against the bed, looking at him with wide eyes.

"I think we will talk this over," he said. He walked slowly toward her.

The flask dropped to the floor. She shrank back.

He paused and smiled. "Or perhaps you would prefer to finish your drink."

The complete story of shock-mystery will be told by John D. MacDonald in his novel—"Blood of the Vixen"—in the next issue.

they can't stop you in the Armored Cavalry!

HISTORY'S greatest heroes ride with you in spirit in the U. S. Army's glory-covered Armored Cavalry. It's the fastest moving, hardest hitting combat team in the world.

You ride in the great tradition of Jeb Stuart and Phil Sheridan. But you move twice as fast and hit ten times as hard. You inherit the mantle of Patton's incomparables who swept across Africa, broke the line at St. Lo and hurled shattering thunderbolts at the heart of Nazidom.

The Armored Cavalry offers big jobs for big men. Not big in size alone. But big in courage and brains. Men who can take it, who crave the excitement,

high adventure and fast-moving life of this proud fighting outfit.

You're more than a soldier in the Armored Cavalry. You're Artilleryman, Infantryman, Tanker and Cavalryman—with the hardest hitting qualities of all four.

If you have a talent for motors and guns, if you like action, if you want to learn leadership, this is the job for you. High pay. Good food and quarters. Travel opportunities. A chance to further your education.

Visit your U. S. Army and U. S. Air Force Recruiting Station:

Death Is

Was this lovely, smoky-eyed girl really his wife? Or was she Anne's twin sister—the tempestuous and evil-souled Zelda—biding her time until her next murder...

Their quarreling hit a murderous pitch. . . .

Exciting Shock-Mystery Novel

a Dame

By Frederick C. Davis

CHAPTER ONE

Death's Twin

THE elevator stopped automatically, and Dayne left the gilt-and-green cage with an anxiously curious glance at the detective who was steering him along from the rear. Kirk nodded and they climbed the steep twist of iron stairs to the roof.

They were apparently at their destination now, on the high roof with its terraced garden and pink stucco penthouse. Kirk had not uttered a word of explanation since they had left the Flamenco

Club, where Dayne had been working up his new dance routine. Now the sober-faced detective said merely:

"You'll have to go in, Mr. Dayne. You'd better get yourself set for a jolt."

"A jolt? Why should I?" Foss Dayne looked hard at Kirk. "What's in there?"

Kirk shook his head. Whatever was in there, he wanted it to hit Dayne cold. Dayne lifted his chin and thrust the penthouse door open.

First he heard a woman's husky exclamation, made half in relief, half in friendly anxiety. "Foss, they found you!"

He had entered a small vestibule, facing a closed door, with a second door open on his right and giving into a small, expensively tricked-out "den." The voice had come from there—the familiar worn voice of Joyce Lane.

She was moving toward him, the usual paleness of her fine face making her hair seem a shinier black, her lips a more vivid red. Dayne—he and his wife Anne both —had been friendly with Joyce for years now—or perhaps it was the other way around; perhaps Joyce had built up this friendship with them. He was startled to see her here in this strange hideaway in the sky; yet it wasn't really surprising at all. More and more, lately, it had seemed to him that wherever he might turn, Joyce appeared at his elbow—a lovely presence, an electrical nearness which he tried to shrug off—and couldn't.

"Foss—Foss, darling, they wouldn't let me phone you. The police, I mean. I wanted to warn you—it's not a pretty thing to walk in on. I know, because I'm the one who found them like that."

"Found them?" Foss Dayne echoed, mystified still.

Joyce was wearing last night's evening dress—a full-skirted blue, dark as midnight, with a tiny star twinkling out here and there, like a facet of its wearer's beauty. Her jet-black hair was glossy as a raven's wing, and perfectly neat, even

though she'd evidently spent the night at the backstage party at the Bandbox Theatre. Foss Dayne and Anne had been there too, but had left earlier than most. Finally leaving the party herself, then, very early this morning, the restless Joyce had dropped in here at this penthouse and found—what?

Dayne repeated, "Them?"

Sergeant Kirk had turned the knob of the other door and now he pushed it open. Joyce stiffened and Dayne stood still, gazing into a lavish living room.

Lavish and garish both. Pure Hollywood in technicolor, this penthouse studio. Soft couches, concealed lights, fur rugs, a built-in-bar, a non-stop phonograph obviously loaded with heart-softening melodies of the *Parlez Moi D'Amour* variety. All the trimmings were there, with something extra very recently added.

The something extra was death.

From where he stood Dayne could see the dead man. Wearing dark trousers and a white shirt, he lay face down on the floor. A bottle—evidently he had been holding it when the bullets struck him in the face—had shattered beside him, mixing his lost blood with premium Scotch. He was a smooth, well-curried corpse. No doubt it would have pleased his vanity if he could have seen how little the process of getting murdered had mussed him up.

"This is his place—or was, Mr. Dayne," Sergeant Kirk said. "Recognize him?"

"Steve Squire. Knew him slightly, just as I know thousands of other night-crawling characters who haunt the hot-spots." Dayne shook his head. "Who did this to him?"

"We think," Kirk answered quietly, "*she* did. The woman over there in the corner. Not so long ago, either—they're both still warm."

"Woman?" Dayne echoed tensely.

"Over there," Kirk repeated. "We

figure she shot him during a liquored-up scrap—using the gun he kept here—then killed herself."

FOSS DAYNE stepped into the room, stiffening himself. He saw now the other squad men and homicide dicks putting the details of the scene on record with camera and notebooks. Kirk preceded Dayne to a spot behind the door where a sheet was spread over a huddled form, and gently dragged the cover off— and Dayne, frozen, started down into a face that was lovely even in death.

She lay in graceful repose, her honey-colored hair a glistening pillow, her eyes open but not staring—smoky green eyes gazing up at nothingness, seeing it a little sadly. Her soft coral-red lips were parted as if to murmur a reluctant farewell. Three strands of pearls encircled her lovely white throat, in stunning contrast to the rich maroon dress with its sweeping V. Her skirt had swirled beautifully as she fell, revealing her gorgeous legs. On one ankle, a diamond anklet twinkled. . . .

The jarring note was the blood caked around the dark hole in her forehead and the revolver lying near her delicate, scarlet-nailed hands.

Sergeant Tom Kirk was saying, "As a matter of formality, Mr. Dayne, will you identify her for us?"

He drew a slow, deep breath. His first glimpse of her had been a jolt, yes—one jarring him down to his dancing toes. For one ghastly instant he had been uncertain; but then he had felt a surging sense of sureness and relief. This couldn't, after all, be Anne—not his wife. Everything about this girl was too gaudy for Anne— and Anne would never be here in this penthouse hideaway of a notorious rounder like Squire. . . .

"Yes, I can identify her," Dayne answered, finding his voice after that brief but chilling shock. "She was my sister-in-law. She was Zelda Sequard—my wife's twin sister."

*　*　*

Now, hours later in his own apartment, he sat facing a lovely girl whose hair was a soft honey-colored glow, whose smoky green eyes watched him intently, whose coral-red lips were parted a little as she listened. She had tucked her slender ankles under her and in the long tapering fingers of one hand she held an emptied wine glass. She wore a dark, plain suit; but otherwise, in every line and detail, she appeared to be the same girl he had seen lifeless on the floor of Steve Squire's penthouse.

But of course she was not. She was the dead girl's twin sister.

"Anne," Foss Dayne said quickly, noticing her empty glass, "let me get you more sherry."

She brought herself quickly to her feet. "Never mind, Foss, darling. I'll get it for myself." To the others she added, "Please go on. Tell me the rest about Zelda, no matter how horrible and shocking it is. I'll hate every word of it in the papers, but there's no use trying to escape the truth of what happened. After all, we're grown up enough to take it."

Joyce Lane smiled—still lovely and trim in last night's gown. "I hope so, Anne. Because it's going to be pretty rough."

Foss Dayne gave her a quick frown; and they were quiet again, watching Anne, tall and blonde and graceful as she moved to the buffet.

This was the Dayne apartment, a small one, showing Anne's tidy taste in the furnishings and decorations. Coming here from the penthouse with Sergeant Kirk and Joyce—of course Joyce—and finding that Anne had returned, Dayne had broken the news as gently as he could.

Anne had said simply:

"You know, Foss, I've been afraid of something terrible, like this, for a long time now—and here it is."

Dayne had expected her to go to pieces under the shock of her sister's scandalous death, and he admired the grip she'd taken on herself—particularly the game way she had faced Sergeant Kirk and answered his countless questions. The sergeant, seeming inclined to make it a little rougher than necessary, kept frowning at his notes and showing an inexplicable reluctance to leave.

Joyce asked him with characteristic boldness, "What's bothering you, Tommy?" She had known him only a few hours now, and strictly officially at that, but she was never one to curtsy to formality. "It's just what it seems to be, isn't it? A fine, juicy case of murder, suicide and high-class debauchery?"

Sergeant Kirk rose, his lips twisted, saying nothing again—on his guard against Joyce, as well he might be.

"After all, it was in the cards, Tommy —wasn't it?" Joyce insisted, her dark eyes studying him. "There was Zelda, in Squire's plushy love-nest, as the tabloids will certainly call it, with each of them two-timing the other. Sooner or later it was bound to explode—especially with Zelda being just the kind to flare up in a jealous alcoholic rage. You might say it turned out the only way it could. Inevitable. Wouldn't you say that, my talkative Tommy?"

"Sure, that's it. The wages of sin is death, sure." Kirk grinned briefly. "Thanks, Mr. and Mrs. Dayne, for cooperating—and my sympathies. I hope I won't have to see you about it again. So long now."

IT WAS Joyce who hurried to let him out of Anne's and Foss's apartment. She came back looking darkly thoughtful. Anne had returned to her chair with her filled glass. Foss had begun pacing up and down.

"How come I didn't know this was building up?" he said. "This pretty little affair between Zelda and Squire, I mean. Was Zelda's taste improving—was she keeping this one under wraps for a change?" He went on, "I can't get used to it—the enormous difference between Zelda and you, Anne. Identical twin sisters—the two of you looked exactly alike —yet inside you were as far apart as heaven and hell."

Anne said softly, "No, that isn't quite true, Foss. We were exactly alike in our inner selves, too. But because Zelda's upbringing was so different from mine, she let her emotions storm out, while I learned to keep mine under control."

Dayne nodded as he went on pacing. He could understand that. A fascinating case to study, these twin sisters.

Their mother was an actress, their father a dramatic director. Both were touring in a stock company when the twin girls were born. For a while the babies had followed the tradition of living in their mother's dressing-room trunk; but soon it had become necessary to find homes for them. Their parents had been unable to arrange for their care without separating them. Anne had been placed with an uncle in Ohio, a minister. Zelda had been taken by friends of mercurial fortunes and the temperaments of gamblers, breeders of racing horses in Virginia. Anne had been disciplined as a little lady—not a stuffy little angel, but charmingly and naturally well-behaved. Zelda, in contrast, had run as wild as any high-strung colt.

Later, the lure of the stage strong in them both, they had headed for Broadway, and for a time they had shared an apartment. Anne had made a slow, quiet start on a career as a dramatic actress only to give it up willingly in order to devote herself to her new husband, that exciting new dancer Foss Dayne, who, she felt, would soon shine among the great dancing stars of all time.

Zelda's chosen career had been night-club torch-singing incidentally, but chiefly men. Perhaps she had never stopped, or hadn't cared, to ask herself what her objective was. Dayne felt fairly sure, however, that her goal had not been a cold and lonely bed six feet under the graveyard sod—at least not so soon as this.

Joyce said, with a knowing smile, "Tell you the rest about Zelda, did you say? It makes fascinating listening, my fine friend. In fact, Foss, you haven't dreamed the half of it."

Foss halted, turning to her uneasily. "Zelda's romp in that penthouse wasn't all of it?"

"No, my sweet." Joyce gazed at him through her long dark lashes. "Unsuspecting lad, aren't you, Foss? You imagine other people are as naturally decent as you are. You make it seem a fine masculine quality, but not many people are that way, brother—and at the risk of disillusioning you a little more I'll confess that, for example, I'm not one of the few. But compared with little Zelda—" Joyce smiled slowly. "An adventurous lassie, Foss. Curious about life, let's say. Eager to fill her cup to overflowing—not always with stuff as high proof as good rye, either."

Anne sat straighter. "I don't know what you mean, Joyce—and how could you know more about Zelda than I do?"

"My big brother is a busy theatrical producer, remember?" Joyce said smoothly. "I like to spend a lot of time backstage, where the grapevine is always humming. It has carried a lot of choice tidbits of news about our Zelda—stuff I've never told you before because I knew that two guys as nice as you wouldn't like hearing it."

Frowning, Foss asked, "Such as?"

"Such as the time she let you believe she'd gone up to the Catskills for a month of bucolic relaxation. That's not where she really was. Actually you'd have found her putting on two shows nightly down at the Love Apple, that low dive deep in the Village. Shows is the right word for them. She was billed at Gilda, the golden-masked Venus. Stripping just to see what it was like."

Startled, Foss saw Anne staring at Joyce with her soft coral mouth opened a little in dismay.

"That's a fair sample, my sweets," Joyce assured them. "She also went to Rio once. An uninhibited little girl, I'm afraid. Very bad, really. The Squire penthouse was a step upward for her— and the fact that she finally got what was coming to her won't really surprise anyone who knew her as she really was."

Joyce added, "I'm telling you this so you'll understand the blood-spilling a little better. You'd soon hear them from other sources anyway. But even I don't know all of it, pals. There's still more— but I haven't quite been able to tease it out of our close-mouthed friend Tommy— so far."

Anne exclaimed, "The detective? Joyce! Do you actually mean he knew about Zelda *before* this morning?"

"I've a hunch he did, my precious—and officially," Joyce answered wryly. "Judging from his reactions, in fact, I'm pretty sure he knows one or two hidden chapters in her busy life. Zelda must have had a little brush with the law some time earlier —something she didn't noise around. And of course Tommy wasn't spilling it. Not that quiet lad. Not on such short acquaintance, anyway."

FOSS stared at the dead girl's sister; and Anne's green-gray eyes gazed widened and frightened into his.

"So in any case, Anne, dearest, don't weep too many tears over the dear departed Zelda. She had her fun—plenty of it. More of her kind of it than you would want in twenty lifetimes." Joyce smiled her attractive, sophisticated smile. "Or me in, say, four or five."

Anne brought herself to her feet, putting her wine glass aside. "We can't deny it. Zelda was really evil. But she's gone now. We've faced the truth about it—" Anne steadied her shoulders—"and now I want to begin forgetting it. I—I'd like to be alone for a little while, if you won't mind. Please—excuse me."

Foss Dayne hurried to the bedroom door with her. Her fingertips stroked a light caress across his cheek; she smiled, then went quietly in and closed the door behind her. Turning back, he found Joyce wearily picking up her fox jacket—ready at last to leave him alone with Anne. She still wore her dark, cynically amused smile.

"What you said about Zelda and the cops—that really worries me, Joyce. For Anne's sake."

"Then let's hope they'll let it lie, Foss, darling," Joyce said. "These next few days are going to be rough on you both anyway. You'll be hounded unmercifully by stony-hearted reporters and fiends with news cameras. But if I know you—and I do—you'll be out there dancing tonight as usual. The show must go on, and all that noble sort of guff—mustn't it?"

Foss was eyeing her. "Certainly I'll go on tonight. What kind of trouper would I be if I didn't? And why don't I tell you to stay the hell out of my life? You never stop needling me."

"That's because you're such a very upright young fool, my lad," Joyce said. "So *damned* upright!" She laughed ruefully.

"Now listen. It's getting later every day. My famous producer brother will soon have his big new musical all whipped together. He needs a feature dancer for it, but he's looking for a name. But my big brother Jonathan respects my judgment in such things, bless his heart, and a little persuasion on my part about a dancer named Dayne would get you that dazzling spot, my boy."

Dayne shook his head. "No, thanks,

Joyce. There's nothing I'd like better, but if I were good enough for it, or big enough for it, the great Jonathan Lane would pick me on his own. His kid sister wouldn't need to point me out to him. But I've told you a thousand times, Joyce, I don't want to get ahead on pull."

"Especially not mine, because you know I'm not being too damned unselfish about it." Joyce smiled at him wistfully and added, "It would be a lovely billing, darling. Your name in lights actually, for a nice long Broadway run. After that you could bank on Hollywood on your own terms. Everything on your own terms, darling."

"You make it plenty tempting, Joyce." Dayne laughed shakenly. "But I'll get there on merit or not at all."

Joyce narrowed her dark eyes. "Aren't you being too upright for your own good, laddie? You don't want me to nudge you out of your comfortable little rut—your cozy little apartment and your pretty homebody of a wife."

She lifted her shining black head. "You wouldn't risk hurting Anne, not for the whole world. She's so sweet, such a tender, trusting girl. She wouldn't deserve it from you, would she—no matter how much you might deserve it for yourself?" Joyce laughed again, a little bitterly. "Well, she's had a bad shock this morning—maybe that's the answer."

"The answer to what?" Dayne said, his voice sharper. "What are you driving at?"

"Anne has never drunk anything stronger than sherry, remember? So maybe she's changing, Foss—maybe she's becoming a little less the sweet and tender soul you think she is. At any rate, she did pour this for herself. I watched her doing it."

Joyce took up the wine glass that Anne had left on the table and pushed it into Dayne's hesitant hand. Then she turned, trailing her jacket. As she opened the door she said, with a dark glance across her shoulder, "Good night, my noble darling."

As he stared at the amber liquid in the glass—just a few drops of it left—he heard Joyce's high heels ticking away.

Sherry, of course. Anne had always disliked more potent drinks. Foss had never known her to take anything stronger than dry sherry, absolutely never. But as he raised the glass to his nostrils he smelled the drink she had poured for herself and liberally swallowed during their talk. . . . Straight rye.

CHAPTER TWO

Blood Red

THE applause broke more explosively and held longer than Foss Dayne had ever heard it before. He bowed and bowed again in the spotlight while it beat around him like a warm surf.

At last escaping from the glare and threading his way through the crowded tables to his dressing room, he realized that the acclaim was not a tribute to his dancing tonight so much as it was a salute of admiration for him simply for appearing. After the day-long nightmare of aggressive reporters and prying lens men, another headliner would have ducked under cover; but Foss Dayne had faced it through, and now, his last show finished at three in the morning, it was, thank God, all over for now. At last he could go back where he was really needed, back home to Anne.

Not taking time to remove his soft-soled dance shoes and his tails, he ducked out the Flamenco's service entrance. At once the ordeal began—the silent blasts of flash bulbs and reporters crowding at his elbows. Head ducked down, fists thrust deep in his pockets, he strode swiftly along the sidewalk—and heard, gratefully, a voice saying, "Taxi for you, Mr. Dayne.

Here, Mr. Dayne, please get right in."

He ducked through the open door, escaping the news hounds—and then discovered Joyce Lane sitting beside him.

Staring at her in resignation—but not entirely displeased—he told himself he should have expected this of her. It was this way with Joyce all the time. She haunted him—a dark ghost in the flesh—and such lovely flesh it was, too. Couldn't she fully realize it was Anne who rated the Number One woman in his life?

"Joyce, my pretty," he said, "there's certainly nothing coy about you; and you're no dope, either; so what makes you think you're not wasting your time?"

"I just keep hoping, darling," she said, smiling at him. "After all, there isn't anything you can do to stop me if I want to be in love with you."

He couldn't ignore the electrical charge these words sent surging into him, but he answered banteringly. "You're a doll in a million, baby, and don't think I'm not flattered; but it isn't quite cricket, is it? I have a very delectable wife very much in the picture, and I'd be a chump to risk losing her."

"You never let me forget her, darling," Joyce said pungently. "But now I'm beginning to have certain doubts about her. They're really special, too, these doubts of mine. Let's talk them over, shall we—seriously?"

Her tone disturbed him, and she didn't explain. She left to him the little formality of directing the driver; and Dayne told him, "Eight-eighteen East Eleventh" —his own apartment, where Anne was waiting for him. Joyce's response to that —since she had a cozy apartment of her own—was a sigh. As the cab veered off, Dayne eyed her.

"About that little incident of the rye," he said. "Anne was under terrific strain —simply didn't notice the difference. Or else she simply wanted to relax her nerves. That's all."

"I'm not so sure." Joyce sounded sobered. "Please, Foss, listen to me. I'm not straining for smart repartee now. This is serious. So serious it scares me." She whispered, "It's really *deadly* serious, Foss."

He said, frowning at her, "It has been deadly enough already."

"But this is worse. It will hit you even harder. If what I think is true—" Joyce's hand closed tightly over his. "I mean every word of it, because it means—danger. Life-and-death danger."

He frowned. "I'll always believe one thing, Joyce. You're pulling for me. In your own womanly way. But danger? Where?"

Her fingers tightened over his. "I've been with Anne this evening, Foss—went to your apartment after you left, so she wouldn't be alone. You see, I was concerned for your honey-haired darling. But when I came away, a little while ago, I wasn't worrying about her any more—not in the same way, at least. Instead, I was anxious for you."

As the taxi swung them down the avenue, he gazed at her hard. "What are you driving at, Joyce? Anxious for me—why?"

"ANNE seems changed, Foss. I know, she was hit by a terrific shock this morning; she's naturally not quite herself now. But I began noticing differences in that girl—strange little changes that can't be accounted for by nervous strain. I mean little mannerisms, small things that might really be much bigger than they seem."

Not understanding this, he let her go on.

"Subtle little changes, Foss. Her mouth, for instance—in repose it used to seem content. Now it seems cynical. Anne used to look at you directly, without self-consciousness. Tonight her eyes were never at rest—they darted here,

there, everywhere, as if incessantly searching. Other things—the way she frowns, her laugh—suddenly they're not the same. There's an entirely different *feeling* in her, Foss. It's as if—" Joyce paused.

Dayne said skeptically. "Go on. Let's have it."

"It's as if she's not the same girl."

The cab had stopped. Foss gazed up at the windows of his apartment. The venetian blinds were drawn; an orchid-tinted glow shone out. Anne was awake, waiting for him, as she always waited up to welcome him home from work.

"Anne's upset worse than she has let on, Joyce," Dayne explained. "You're simply not making allowances."

"Foss," Joyce said earnestly. "Foss, listen. I'm trying to tell you something that will really shake you. You won't want to believe it. But anyway I'm warning you to keep your eyes sharp every minute you're with her. And think it over—think fast."

She drew a deep breath. "Because I've come to believe that girl up there in your apartment—the girl waiting for you now—is not Anne."

"Not Anne!" he blurted. "What are you talking about? Of course she's Anne! Who else could she be?"

Joyce said softly, "Zelda."

He stared at her stunned, then began shaking his head. "I saw Zelda lying dead in that penthouse this morning. I identified her as Zelda to the police. It *was* Zelda, of course."

"You saw a girl who looked exactly like Zelda. An identical twin. And you could have been wrong."

Foss Dayne continued to stare. "Good Lord, Joyce! You're saying you think it was Anne, my wife, instead of Zelda, lying there in Squire's studio, a suicide? She hardly knew Squire by sight. I'm absolutely certain of that. Yet—you say it's Zelda, posing as Anne, that I've been with all day—Zelda pretending to be

Anne, who's upstairs even now? Good Lord, surely I know my own wife!"

"I hope I'm utterly wrong, Foss. I wish it wouldn't keep adding up to the same answer, in my own mind, at least. So for your own sake—and maybe for mine too, because I do love you, remember?—keep those guileless eyes of yours wide open."

"But Joyce—what earthly basis could you have for dreaming up this nightmare?"

"I was coming to that," Joyce went on, her hand still on his. "It goes back to how I happened to find those two dead bodies this morning. I walked in on them like that because Steve Squire had phoned, asking me to drop over."

Frowning up at those softly glowing windows, Dayne asked, "At that hour? You knew Squire that well?"

"No," Joyce answered. "My own taste runs more to the Boy Scout type. He called me because I was as close to Zelda as anyone. He'd grown afraid of her, Foss. They'd quarreled repeatedly and she was drinking like mad. He was afraid that unless some friend of hers took her in hand, she might blow her top. He said he'd tried to get help from Anne but hadn't had an answer from her. Such an affair might be a little too noisome for Anne's sensitive nose, of course."

"Odd Anne never mentioned—"

"A thoughtful angel like Anne wouldn't want to worry you with it, darling. Me, I'm not so subtle. More realistic, let's call me. I'd noticed Zelda on the loose and hitting the bottle hard—always rye—with a glitter in her eye that wasn't to be trusted, so I dropped in on Squire after the party this morning. It seems I was just a little too late. Zelda had already done just what he'd been afraid of, using that gun.

"But there was something wrong in that picture, Foss—a false note from the very start." Joyce stated it with con- viction. "Zelda wouldn't have killed herself. She liked living too much, in her own feverish way. Rather than a bullet in the brain she'd much prefer to take her chances with a jury, I'm sure. She simply was not the suicide type, Foss."

Dayne had begun quietly to laugh.

"LISTEN to me, you well-meaning idiot!" Joyce flared up at him. "Can't you see it now? Zelda was drunk and desperate. She had committed murder. She saw a beautiful out—a chance to sidestep the whole thing by posing as her own twin sister—"

Laughing and shaking his head, Dayne said, "This is a very fascinating dream you've whipped up, Joyce, but it's just too far out of this world. Sorry, but I can't stay to hear the rest of it. Anne's waiting for me up there and I'm already late. Good night, my morbid little pretty."

Joyce sprang from the taxi after him, grasped his arm, stopped him. "I expected you to laugh it off this way, Foss. You just can't understand how evil other people can be. But don't forget what I've said. Watch her! Please, don't dare forget it for a single minute!"

He detached her clinging hand, shaking his head and chuckling. "Oh, really, Joyce." Aware of her gazing after him, but not glancing back, he hurried inside.

When he buzzed at the door of his apartment, on the tenth floor, the door was opened wide after a moment's delay and Anne, wearing a sunshine-yellow housecoat, came quickly into his arms.

"Foss, darling," she murmured. "So glad you're back. So lonely without you."

Lifting his head a little, to gaze past the honey-tinted glimmer of her hair, he saw a faint haze floating in the air.

"Smoke?" he said. "Someone's been smoking? You, Anne? But you never liked it before."

She stiffened, backed away and laughed briefly. "I still don't Foss. Just thought

I'd try it again, to see if it would ease my nerves a little. But it didn't—just left a bad taste in my mouth."

She went on quickly, "Did the show go well? You look tired. No wonder. I'm tired too, darling. It's been such a ghastly day. Do you mind if I go right to bed, now that you're home at last?"

"You shouldn't have waited up for me, sweet," he said. "Hustle right along."

She kissed his cheek. "You're such a nice guy. Good night, darling."

He watched her as she went into the bedroom, a beautiful figure with her yellow hair fluffed above her yellow, snugly draped robe. A slight frown darkened his face as he gazed around the living room. There was pungency in the air. Liquor. Yes, rye. Rye, the stuff Anne never touched but Zelda always chose. And the ash-tray. It was crammed full of butts stained with lip rouge. But of course, Foss Dayne reminded himself, Joyce had been here with Anne for hours. . . .

With a smile Dayne turned to the bedroom door. Married these four years to Anne, he still took pleasure in watching her slip into bed. She did it with such natural grace—sliding her small feet from her slippers, whirling her robe off, then hanging it neatly on a hook, giving her lovely long body a last luxurious stretch with her long nightgown swinging at her toetips, then flying under the blanket as lightly as a ballerina. All of it was so beautifully characteristic of Anne—the neatness of the hung robe, each movement airily, flowingly smooth.

Dayne watched through the door as she paused beside one of the twin beds—and something completely unexpected startled him. Tonight she didn't ease lightly from her slippers—she kicked them at random across the room. She didn't hand the robe, but let it drop carelessly on the floor.

He stood there motionless, a chill sneaking into his blood. She twiddled her fingers at him and murmured drowsily, " 'Night, darl-ing."

As she lay there with her eyes closed he went closer slowly, the frost growing sharper on his nerves, and gazed at her hand reposing in the soft light. As long as he had known Anne he had avoided personal garishness—had, for one thing, used nail polish of a light shell-pink tint. But the hand lying on the coverlet now had nails lacquered a vivid blood red.

CHAPTER THREE

Poison of Doubt

THE slow, even rhythm of her breathing was the only sound in the room. The early murky gray of an overcast day hung outside the windows, and in its dimness Foss Dayne, raised on one elbow, gazed in unbelieving fascination at the girl in the other bed—and felt the nettles of an uncertain anxiety which he could not stifle.

While she slept he had lain there painfully awake during all the dark hours, telling himself over and over that this notion of Joyce's was fantastic. The strange changes that she had noticed in Anne were only natural under such unnerving circumstances.

After all, too, Anne had explained them away in a few words. What was Joyce trying to do—go so far as to poison his mind against his wife with sly, baseless suspicions? If so, it was a raw trick—damned underhanded of her to try to take unfair advantage of Anne at a time when she was suffering a nasty shock and was hardly herself.

Hardly herself. . . .

Foss Dayne argued with himself in this dogged way, with a frown for Joyce, as he gazed at the yellow hair glistening on the pillow of the next bed. And again, in spite of himself, his eyes shifted to the slender hand resting on the blanket—the hand with the nails a bright scarlet which Anne had never before worn.

Suddenly Dayne swung his legs down and rose. The girl in the other bed remained quiet as he dressed. While she still slept he let himself out of the apartment. He had made a decision—to stop letting himself be nagged by such gnawing uncertainties—to check and make sure for himself, as far as possible, just what the facts actually were.

He strode rapidly along busy streets. Although it was an unusually early hour for a night-club dancer to be up and about, millions of others were hustling to start their working day. Dayne threaded his way through them nimbly, until, slowing in a side street, he paused to face an ornate doorway that bore in gold the name of *Kimball Mortuary.*

Dayne stepped into a reception room where a certain brisk businesslike air mingled with the atmosphere of a chapel. A black-garbed man left his desk with a smile to come over to Foss Dayne.

"Good morning, Mr. Dayne. I'd intended phoning you a little later in the morning to say we've overcome the difficulties I mentioned to Mrs. Dayne the last time she phoned. The arrangements are now completed for the service this afternoon."

"This afternoon," Dayne repeated softly, taken by surprise. It was sooner than he had expected—sooner than Anne had mentioned.

"Yes, we've managed to hurry it up a bit, just as Mrs. Dayne wished," the mortician said. "Two o'clock. Would you like to go over the details with me, Mr. Dayne?"

"No, I'll leave all that to—my wife." He was disturbed despite himself at Anne's surprising, almost stealthy haste. "I came to see my sister-in-law's body. For only a moment," he added. "Privately."

"Certainly, Mr. Dayne."

Kimball escorted him down a hush-filled hallway to a door. There he paused, bowing Dayne into a small room where the lights were amber and the scent of flowers heavy. Alone, he stepped to a couch where—

It shocked him again. The same sunshine-yellow hair sparkling on, this time, a pillow of blue satin—the sort of pillow on which only the dead slumber. The same oval face in repose, its sweetness seeming, this time, to be untouched by any slight hint of worldliness. The undertaker had skillfully removed all the caked blood, had concealed all traces of that ugly bullet hole in her forehead, so that the resemblance was all the more startling now. Perfectly, exactly like the girl sleeping in his apartment—sleeping a shorter sleep than this. And her hands?

Gently Dayne lifted the satin shroud. It revealed the dead hands, beautifully delicate, crossed in a gesture of eternal rest. And her nails were—bright scarlet.

Of course! Unquestionably, then, this really was Zelda, just as Dayne had believed at first. The scarlet enamel on Anne's nails at the moment was another of those trivial details that she could explain away with a word, in half a moment. . . . It *was* Anne sleeping now in her bed, at home, and the dead girl here *was* Zelda. Of course. . . .

Foss Dayne sensed a soft step behind him. He turned to see that a quiet-mannered young man had appeared in the doorway—Sergeant Tom Kirk.

"'Morning, Mr. Dayne. Didn't mean to disturb you," Kirk said respectfully. "We're both in circulation pretty early today, aren't we?"

Dayne moved toward the detective. Kirk stepped back from the doorway politely, as if to let him pass; but Dayne paused.

"What interests you here, Sergeant? There's nothing left in this case officially. Is there?"

Kirk smiled slowly. "You'll have to excuse a cop for having a doubting mind, Mr. Dayne. It's our business to be suspicious. Nothing in it this time, I guess—but I keep wondering why Zelda Sequard seemed to forget, all of a sudden, at the last minute, how beautiful she was."

"Forget? How?"

"A woman's beauty is highly important to her, Mr. Dayne. Even when she gets to the point of destroying her own life she's still not willing to destroy her good looks. That's why, almost invariably, a woman uses poison or gas. But Zelda used a gun—fired the bullet spang into the middle of her nice high forehead—messed herself up. Well, maybe she didn't care any more—maybe that's why she was an exception to the rule. But I just keep wondering, Mr. Dayne, that's all."

Dayne said tensely, "Wondering whether she was really a suicide, you mean?"

KIRK looked straight at him. "I didn't say that. But if it wasn't what it appeared to be—if it was actually a double murder, with somebody plugging *both* Squire and the girl and then rigging her to look like a suicide—that would explain certain puzzling things about it, Mr. Dayne. And it would also keep me interested in the case."

Dayne stood still, shaken by the return of his deepest doubts. Kirk's very quietness chilled him. The detective disappeared into the reception room beyond, and Dayne turned to stare again at the girl lying dead on the flower-banked couch.

Anne! In one instant of stabbing grief Dayne thought wildly that if this dead girl were actually Anne—if his Anne were actually a victim of murder—

There he checked his riotous thoughts, clenched his fists hard in his pockets and forced himself to leave that room of blossom-scented death.

Kirk was not in the reception room when he strode through and out into the street, but he felt hauntedly that he had not seen the last of Kirk. He kept telling himself as he strode along the sidewalk that the whole picture—as both Joyce's notion and Kirk's tenuous theory had it—was fantastic. He ordered himself heatedly to quit thinking about it. He damned well couldn't go on this way, questioning Anne—actually questioning her identity, her very existence—over nothing.

When he let himself into his apartment he was greeted by the familiar, reassuring odors of coffee bubbling in the percolator and bread browning in the toaster. Anne was up and busy. She heard his step and came hurrying from the kitchenette.

She was barelegged, her small feet in fluffy slippers; a bright-colored peasant apron over her swingy skirt. Her lovely hair was tumbled high on her head, as she always wore it first thing in the morning—beautifully casual. Her bright smile, she ran into his arms.

"It frightened me, darling, to wake up and find you gone!"

In spite of himself he found himself puzzling, even as he held her close. Was it Anne speaking? It was her voice, of course—just as Zelda's voice would have seemed to be Anne's—but those words she'd spoken. Weren't they a little *too* wall-flowerish? Anne wasn't given to being silly about such things. Waking up and finding Foss's bed empty, she'd have realized at once, in a commonsense way, that Foss had most probably gone out for an early walk.

"Frightened to find you gone. . . ." Were these Anne's words really—or those of someone skillfully but not quite perfectly impersonating her?

Dayne found himself holding one of her hands, frowning at her long crimson nails.

"Terrible, aren't they, darling?" he heard her saying. "I ran out of my favorite color several days ago—not a single drop of it left—and I just happened to have a bottle of this brilliant red stuff that somebody gave me for Christmas years ago. Awful, isn't it? I'll get more of my regular tint next time I go shopping." She kissed him suddenly. "Breakfast ready in a few minutes, darling."

She pressed her lips over his again, lingeringly this time, and with their warmth he felt a great surge of reassurance. It was just as he had promised himself—Anne had made it seem so entirely natural, had banished those prodding demons from his mind. Suddenly everything was right again—perfect as it had always been between them. It seemed utterly ridiculous now that he had ever seriously considered the slightest doubt of his one-and-only Anne.

"Be right with you, honey," he sang out, and he stepped into the bedroom.

Slipping off his coat, he froze. There on Anne's vanity he saw a small bottle sitting among flacons of perfume. The small one was the familiar size used for nail enamel. The color of the enamel was not the scarlet that Anne had worn last night, not the same glaring red she was wearing now. Instead, it was the pale-tint called "naturelle."

Anne had said, "Not a single drop of it left, darling." But the bottle wasn't empty. It was more than half full!

Foss Dayne stood very still, held there by a dread that broke through all his defenses. It was a thought that hit him with a more shattering impact than anything that Joyce or Kirk had said. He found himself thinking—as he felt the sting of terror—*If what they say is true, then Anne is dead—my Anne has been killed—and the woman who is here with me now is her murderer!*

CHAPTER FOUR

To Live With Murder

SHE paused at the door—Anne in every lovely line, so far as his eye could detect. She was sliding her hands into Anne's black gloves. She wore Anne's smartest black hat, Anne's jacket of shaggy black fur, Anne's gossamer nylons and shiny black sling-back pumps. It was impossible for Foss Dayne to believe she was not Anne—yet even as she spoke to him in Anne's voice his torturing doubts would not let him be certain of her.

"Won't be gone long, Foss, darling. Just a short walk for a little fresh air. I'll be back in plenty of time for Zelda's funeral service."

"I'll wait here, then," he said. "Good-by—Anne."

He watched the door closing, heard her high heels clicking down the hall, then the elevator humming. He turned to the windows that opened on a shallow little balcony that was more decorative than useful.

Leaning out, he watched the entrance of the building ten stories below. He saw her appear, hurry along to the corner, then turn and vanish.

He straightened, his face set, and said half aloud, "Now, damn it, I'll do something about this. I'll settle it somehow. There's got to be some sort of answer right here—and I'm going to find it."

He strode into the bedroom, to the corner where Anne's closet door stood open, where her vanity sat. The inner nook of the apartment knew Anne more intimately than any other. Here he should be able to discover some small item to settle his unbearable doubt. So far, after hours of listening to her and watching her, he still didn't know. Each time, just when he had told himself that certainly this *was* Anne, new suspicions had risen to mock him. Every dubious question could be given a glib answer—and yet they remained as haunting doubts. *He still did not know.*

How could he make sure? So far he had thought of no entirely reliable way. He was hunting for one now, here in this corner of the bedroom; he was determined to find one before she returned. That damned bottle of nail polish, for example, proved nothing, really. Pointed out to her, she would have said, probably, "Why, yes! There it was, all the time—how ever did I overlook it?" And he would have to leave the point right there, in unanswerable uncertainty.

Now he grasped an opportunity to probe into her closet. Five minutes of that got him nowhere. Every single garment here was, of course, Anne's—and every one of them a perfect fit for Anne's twin sister also. There was nothing here which he definitely could say was not Anne's but Zelda's—absolutely nothing.

He turned next to her vanity and poked into the small drawers, among handkerchiefs and ribbons and neatly rolled stockings. Again he found nothing—until his fingers felt a hard object hidden under scented lace in the rear of the lower drawer. He brought up the thing, staring at it in disbelief. *An automatic.*

It was his own gun, a Luger, a souvenir of a visit into the interior of Europe via the Normandy beachhead. Back home as a civilian, he had been accorded the official courtesy of a license for it. But he hadn't expected to find it here in Anne's vanity. He had kept it in a box on his closet shelf, out of harm's way. But now —here within Anne's quick reach—*and loaded*—

If he should ask her about it, what answer would he get? "Why, let me see, Foss, darling. Oh, yes, it was the week you played Boston. Months ago! I stayed here, remember, with a bad cold? I was frightened one night—rumors of a prowler in the building. I just thought I'd better have your gun handy. Silly of me, I know, with the door safely bolted and all that. Afterward I just forgot all about it."

So easy to explain away—yet so chillingly reminiscent of the gun in Squire's penthouse—a gun used to blast out two lives not so many hours ago.

Foss Dayne dropped the clip from the automatic's butt and stripped it of its load of cartridges. He dropped them into pocket, seated the emptied clip again and returned the gun to its hiding place in the drawer. Then having done it, he felt foolish and guilty, as if he had committed a small act of faithlessness against a wife who didn't deserve it.

But he pressed on with his purpose, looking intently for proof or disproof, whichever it might be. His search took him now into the living room, to the desk where Anne kept her household accounts and answered her mail. He opened a packet of letters and found them to be notes of a social nature, of no consequence. Then, separated from the others and tucked away under the blotter, he uncovered two others. Both were typed awkwardly; and the first began:

Dear Mrs. Dayne,
  I don't like to write you about a matter as personal as this, but I haven't been able to catch you at home or on the phone. I guess you and I circulate at different times of the day and night. Anyway it's about your sister Zelda. She's getting to be too hot-headed to handle and it's time she got cooled off, if only for her own good. If I could talk to you about her, Mrs. Dayne, and if you could get her to go away for a while, maybe up in the country somewhere—

In cold astonishment Dayne skipped to the signature: *Steve Squire.*

ANNE hadn't mentioned these notes to Foss. Had this been because she had taken time first to earnestly think the situation over?

Squire's second note, pressing the matter, made clear that he still felt Anne was the one best able to help:

Dear Mrs. Dayne,
  I can't blame you for wanting to avoid getting mixed up in such a mess as this, but I thought you would be the best bet to steer your sister away from the real trouble she's heading into unless—

The rasping note of the door buzzer interrupted. Dayne rose, scanning the rest of the second note, and felt that Anne could not have ignored Squire's appeal. It had been sent by Special Delivery early yesterday morning, only a few hours before murdering bullets had knocked Squire's last drink from his hand.

Shaken again, Dayne thrust Squire's notes into his coat pocket as he opened the entrance. Joyce Lane and Sergeant Tom Kirk came in quickly, unbidden, and shut the door firmly behind them.

"Foss," Joyce said breathlessly, "where is she? Do you know?"

"Of course I know," Dayne answered impatiently. "She went out for a walk."

"She walked, all right, laddie, but do you know where?" Joyce said quickly. "To a place on Third Avenue run by a man named Krona, an undertaker. That's where Steve Squire's body was taken after it was carted out of the morgue."

"*Squire's* body?"

"She went there for a last regretful look at her boy friend. Right now she's sitting inside a bar on Lex, trying hard not to soak up too much rye before the start of the funeral services. And don't tell me I dreamed up this part. Tommy tailed her all the way, and I went right along."

Dayne stared at them. "But I keep telling you, Ann can't be expected to act entirely normal at a time like this. Anything she might do now, upset as she is, is no proof—"

"Foss, we know it's not conclusive proof," Joyce broke in. "That's what we're hunting for—something to clinch it. Because, meanwhile, you're in terrible danger."

Foss Dayne thought of that automatic hidden in the vanity drawer. He kept a grim grip on himself as Kirk cut in:

"Exactly, Mr. Dayne. Now, think this one over hard before you answer it—it's plenty important. Do you know of any way, any way at all, of telling those twin sisters apart?"

After a long moment of strained silence Dayne said, "No. There is no sort of mark, no scar or blemish that only one of them has and not the other. Physically they have always been exactly alike. But there have been certain differences between them—such as background, experience, general attitude—"

Joyce said quickly. "Exactly the sort of things I noticed—the little differences that make me *sure* this girl is really Zelda and not Anne. . . . Tommy, give him the rest."

Kirk nodded gravely. "I've got a statement from an assistant janitor at the building where Squire lived. This bird isn't bright enough to figure what happened upstairs, but he knows what he saw.

He said—get this—that while he was sweeping the sidewalk this morning Miss Sequard went in twice but only came out once."

Joyce took it up. "What he actually saw, Foss, was one twin going in, then the other. The one who came out seemed to be Anne—and the one who didn't come down stayed up there dead."

Dayne's throat was tight and dry. "Anne hasn't mentioned going up there. . . . "

"Because she's dead, Foss. Anne is dead." Both Joyce firsts were clenched white. "This girl who has been here with you is *not* Anne!"

KIRK went on: "Better take a good clear look at it, Mr. Dayne. Zelda was there in that penthouse with Squire. They were liquored up. Their quarreling hit a murderous pitch, with Zelda grabbing Squire's gun and blasting him down. Then Ann came in. She came in and found Zelda and the dead man.

"Remember Zelda had gone berserk, crazy with drink. She was grasping about in selfish desperation for some way, any way, to get out of this murder mess. Anne, as a witness, made it worse for her. In a panic already, she must have gone to pieces a second time. A few words from Anne would have been enough to set her off again, even to the extent of shooting down her own sister. Then, once Anne was killed, Zelda saw that her dead sister was her way out."

Joyce took it up. "The substitution was easy for Zelda to fix, Foss. A few little characteristic touches to make Ann seem to be Zelda—then hurrying back here to take the place of the sister she had killed. . . .

"Remember, Zelda and Anne didn't always live apart; they shared an apartment for a while. What's more, Zelda had hundreds of opportunities to observe Anne as your wife when she dropped in on you.

Especially considering the acting talent in her blood, she was perfectly able to step into Anne's shoes and fool even you—for a time, at least. But she had to guard against only one small danger to her masquerade—little lapses of habit, the very things I began to notice, Foss. . . . Please, for your own sake, Foss, can't you see it now?"

Dayne braced himself against their earnestness. "I still say you haven't one bit of proof—"

Kirk was silent for a moment, gazing intently at Dayne.

"No, no proof," Kirk said softly. "That was the trouble before. You see, yesterday's murder wasn't her first."

It rocked Dayne. "Not the first!"

"No. You remember the Cason case several years ago in Connecticut? Big broken. Suicide by monoxide—or so the papers had it. And the Blighton case last year, the drug manufacturer. Suicide again, by gun this time. The papers played both cases down. Convincing enough, both pictures—except for an odd coincidence. Both Cason and Blighton—like Squire—were mixed up with a hot-blooded babe named Zelda Sequard."

Dayne felt Joyce's dark eyes fixed on him as Kirk softly went on: "We couldn't prove anything either time, Mr. Dayne. Sure, we have a scientific lab and plenty of special sensitive tests, but more often than not they're no practical good. We were morally sure the babe had done it both time, but we lacked evidence and couldn't touch her legally. So I've been waiting for her to show in another rigged-up suicide, and yesterday she did. Her own this time—apparently. Well, Mr. Dayne, I think three are enough. I don't want her staging a fourth suicide. Not when it's too likely to be that of a guy named Foss Dayne."

Dayne said, from a painfully dry throat, "But why—why me?"

"Because the day is sure to come when

you'll stop making allowances for her, Foss!" Joyce said forcefully. "Once this scandalous little affair dies down, she should return to being her old self. But she won't—not quite. There will be unavoidable differences. They'll bother you. You'll begin to wonder—and sooner or later, Foss, you'll have to be silenced." She burst out at him, "Damn it all, Foss, you've got to see it—I don't want to lose you!"

He frowned at them, licking his lips. "What do you want me to do?"

"Help us fine proof," Kirk said emphatically. "A test—something really decisive. Can you do it?"

Dayne walked over to the window and stood looking out, thinking of Anne and the girl who looked so much like her..... At last he turned.

"All right," he said. "Heaven knows I want this thing settled. . . ."

"There isn't much time, Foss," Joyce said. "She'll be coming back any minute now. Tell us—is there any way?"

Dayne nodded. "Yes, there's a way. I'm keeping it under my hat—but you can help, Joyce. You and your big brother Jonathan, the celebrated producer."

Dayne smiled wryly. "Ask him to phone here in an hour or so, when Anne is reasonably sure to be here. This is Saturday, so have him invite us out to his place in Westport for the weekend. He'll probably be working late at the theatre, staging his new musical, and he'll pick us up at Grand Central. We'll all catch the last train together after my last show tonight. That's all, Joyce. I'll handle the rest right here—alone with Anne."

Kirk asked, "Are you sure it will work, Mr. Dayne? A slip-up, you know, could be—fatal."

"I'm certain enough," he answered. "It will satisfy you as to whether she's Zelda or Anne—and me, too." Dayne forced a smile. "We'll all know then for sure . . ."

Kirk nodded. "You're doing the right

thing, Mr. Dayne." He turned briskly to the door.

Joyce hurried after him but paused. Dayne's pulse quickened as she gazed back at him in silent anxiety. She had never seemed lovelier, never more audaciously forthright. . . .

Then he shut the door—and alone now, bracing himself to meet the test, he drew a breath laden with dread.

CHAPTER FIVE

Devil's Trial

THREE-THIRTY a. m. In the living room of the Dayne apartment an overnight bag sat near the door, packed and ready to go. Near it stood the girl whom Foss Dayne had watched so quietly and carefully these long hours.

All during the funeral service in the Kimball chapel, and during the burial also, he had kept himself keenly aware of her every move and gesture. Over and over again he had told himself, "She's Anne—of course she's Anne. Now that the strain is letting up she's more her natural self."

He had felt a steady lifting of his heart until now he was almost blithe in his reassurance, inwardly laughing at himself for the foolish way he had worried. Gazing at this blonde girl standing in willowy loveliness near the door, he told himself he had been a fool to doubt her.

"It was so thoughtful of Jonathan Lane to invite us, Foss — especially since we don't know him at all well." She smiled as she drew on her long black gloves. "Joyce fixed it for us, I'm sure. I know we'll have a heavenly time. They're such charming people, and it will be such a marvelous chance to — forget. . . . All ready to go, Foss?"

He stepped into the bedroom, out of her sight, his smile fading. He wasn't going to like these next few minutes; but he couldn't dodge them. It was imperative; he had to make absolutely certain, if for no other reason than to prove to Kirk and Joyce how wrong he was now sure they were. He was going to do it thoroughly, for Anne's sake—banish every possible doubt now and forever. In a very short time now it would be entirely settled—all fears destroyed, only happiness ahead.

He hummed a snatch of a song as he made his first planned move—to Anne's vanity. He drew the lowest drawer open noiselessly, slid his hand deep into the rear of it. But then he stiffened. The gun—the automatic he had left where he had found it hidden under the lacy handkerchiefs—was gone.

The gun—gone. . . .

Her voice reached him from the living room. "We'll have to hurry, or we'll miss our host and the train, too, darling."

"Coming," he said quickly. "In just a second—Anne."

He returned to the living room, coldly puzzled. The missing gun, startling as it was, could wait for an explanation. It brought him a shudder, but it was not the crucial thing. He had another question to ask—the all-important one—and only a few moments left for it. He paused, gazing at her in teetering silence.

"All set now, darling?" she asked, smiling.

"All set, except—" With a twinge in his heart he forced himself to add it—"except for one thing."

"Yes, Foss?"

This was it. This was the moment he still dreaded in spite of all his gnawing reassurances. He felt he was about to do a sneaking thing, yet it was inescapable. . . . This was it.

"The knife, Anne."

She gazed at him with her smoky-green eyes, her coral-red lips curved a little in a smile. "The knife, Foss?"

"Yes," he said. "That very special knife from Jonathan Lane's collection, remember? We've got to return it to him, of course."

She stood there near the door, beside a lamp shining into her glimmering honey-golden hair, looking prettily puzzled as he waited for an answer.

"Well, then, Foss," she said, "hustle up Mr. Lane's knife, and let's go, darling."

"But I don't know where it is, Anne," he said. "You'll have to tell me."

She drew her coat snug at her slender throat as if needing its warmth. It *was* a little chilly in the apartment, with the heat lowered for the night, Foss thought. Or perhaps he felt the chill of lurking fear. Why was she hesitating? Why did she seem so bewildered?

"Foss, I'm terribly tired and mixed up. Please don't play a game with me now. Really, darling, I'm not quite sure what you mean."

Play a game? If this could be called a game it was a deadly grim one—with Death taking a hand. Foss tried to appear casual, to conceal the increasing tightness of his nerves as he watched her lips curve in a softly imploring smile.

"I know, Anne, darling, you've been under a terrific strain," he said. "It has been much tougher on you than on me, of course, but I feel it, too—sometimes I'm not quite sure of my own name. But it would be a little embarrassing for us to see Lane without returning his knife —so please try to remember where you put it."

She said hesitantly, "Are—are you sure you're not the one who tucked it away somewhere, Foss?"

He stiffened himself and said, "I'm sure of that, Anne. Shall I tell you how it was? Maybe it will refresh your memory. First, you remember, I'd planned a new number for the Flamenco show—a Mayan dance, very colorful. While I was whipping it together, Joyce brought me this knife. It would make a good publicity angle to play up, she said, because it was a genuine Mayan sacrificial knife, a true museum piece from her brother's collection.

"That was only a few days ago and as it happened, I changed my mind soon afterward about the Mayan thing — chucked it out in favor of my new deep-sea ballet. That left me with the valuable knife which I no longer had any use for. You remember all this, of course, don't you, Anne?"

"Of course, Foss," she said impatiently. "But the rest—"

"The other evening we were here alone together, honey," he went on, watching her sharply. "I was sitting here in this chair, reading. You were over there, somewhere behind me. You said, 'This knife worries me, Foss. It's too valuable to leave lying around, and besides, somebody with a few drinks in him might begin clowning around with it, not realizing it's sharp as a razor. I'm going to put it out of reach until we have a chance to return it.'

"I didn't look around, Anne; I just said, 'That's a smart idea,' while I went on reading. Then you said, 'Now—it will be safe there.' You'd put it somewhere, Anne—but I didn't see where."

He watched her. She said, looking abashed, "Of course, I remember now."

HE DREW a deep breath. Here was the answer he had been praying for. She was recalling something which only Anne in all this world could remember —something of which Zelda would necessarily be completely ignorant. She knew, as only Anne could know!—and that one little certainty was enough to demolish all his doubts for evermore.

He smiled in dizzy relief.

"Sure you remember! So if you'll just get that knife out from its hiding place,

Anne, we'll be right off to our wonderful weekend."

Pulling her long black gloves tighter, she said, "Please get it for me, darling. There, on the top shelf of the bookcase —far over in the corner. Just reach back in the space behind the books and you'll put your hand right on it."

"Sure thing!" he sang out.

With a happy melody on his lips he swung a chair into the corner beside the window. He stepped up and reached to the topmost shelf. Stretching on the tips of his dancing toes, he slid his hand along behind the books, through dusty emptiness.

"Can't seem to find—"

He paused, still with his lean body stretched up, but looking down over his shoulder at the girl who was standing now in the center of the room. Her eyes were narrowed at him. Her lips, not soft now, were a cruel, vindictive line. One of her gloved hands was lifted, formed into a hard black fist. She had the Luger in a tight grip, aiming it at him with deadly steadiness.

"Don't move, Foss," she said. Her voice was edged. "Not a muscle—darling."

He held himself still there, dizzy with the jolt of it, as the slit-eyed girl came closer.

"It was a test, wasn't it, Foss?" she said, a low, husky note creeping into her voice. "You couldn't let bad enough alone —you had to find out the worse. So now you know, and it's going to cost you. The works. Your life. . . . Damn you, you've forced me to it!"

Holding himself motionless under the threat of the gun, Dayne said, "it will be one time too many."

"I'm not so sure," she answered steadily. "As your grieving widow, I'll have a neat story to tell the police. It will go like

(Please continue on page 95)

Nightmare Man

◆   ◆   ◆

HERMAN WILLIS was a little man. He was little in stature and little in importance to a busy world, just one of the millions of little men who grub at grimy, work-a-day jobs. Herman Willis was a pants presser. A quiet, near-sighted, completely bald little man who asked nothing of the world and of whom the world asked nothing. Yet, the People of the State of New York were going to demand that little Herman Willis be made to pay the Supreme Penalty.

It had been one of those sweltering, hot New York days. Herman had spent nine hours in a cloud of steam over his presser and was glad when it was time to lock up the shop and go home.

He walked up Second Avenue towards Fifty-sixth street, a tired, drooping little figure of a man. As he began to think of the evening ahead, however, the weariness slipped from his shoulders and his step became buoyant. He was anxious to get home to *her*. There was a particularly nice bit of business coming up with *her* tonight—that is, if he could depend upon Mr. Streech. And Mr. Streech had *promised* that he would have it for him tonight.

Herman Willis stopped at a delicatessen and bought ten cents worth of potato salad, a dill pickle, a loaf of rye bread, and fifteen cents worth of cold luncheon meat. In the liquor store next door, he bought a pint bottle of gin. Then he walked up Fifty-sixth Street towards First Avenue.

He stopped under the sidewalk awning of an expensive-looking hotel in the middle of the block, and peered into the cool lobby. The doorman saw him and walked out to him. Herman noticed that he was wearing a new uniform. That was a good

healthy sign—for the business tonight.

"Hello, Herman," the doorman said. He reached in his hip pocket and drew out a handkerchief. Herman watched his hand and flinched with disappointment when he saw only the handkerchief. The doorman wiped his forehead. "Been a hot day, eh, Herman?"

"Yes, Mr. Streech," Herman said. "It's been a steaming hot day."

The doorman laughed and nudged Herman in the ribs. "I get it. You work in steam all day."

Herman watched him wipe his forehead. He wondered whether he was ever going to stop. Back and forth went the handkerchief; under his eyes, under his nose, across his face and around the back of his neck.

The doorman couldn't stand the look of torture in Herman's eyes any longer. "I got it for you, Herman," he whispered. "I tore it off when I turned the old uniform in yesterday. I told them I lost it." He reached in a side pocket and drew out a gold epaulet.

Herman fondled the metallic gold strands and sighed, "I'll never be able to thank you enough, Mr. Streech. I needed it very badly."

The doorman watched Herman cross the street and enter a dismal, yellow-brick tenement house. He smiled expansively and felt that he had done a remarkably good deed. He wondered what Herman was going to do with the epaulet.

As Herman climbed the stairs to his sixth-floor, front apartment, the stench assailed his nostrils. It was the indefinable stench of too many humans crowded in too old tenements, the greasy odors of frying foods blended with the over-all smell left by millions of past

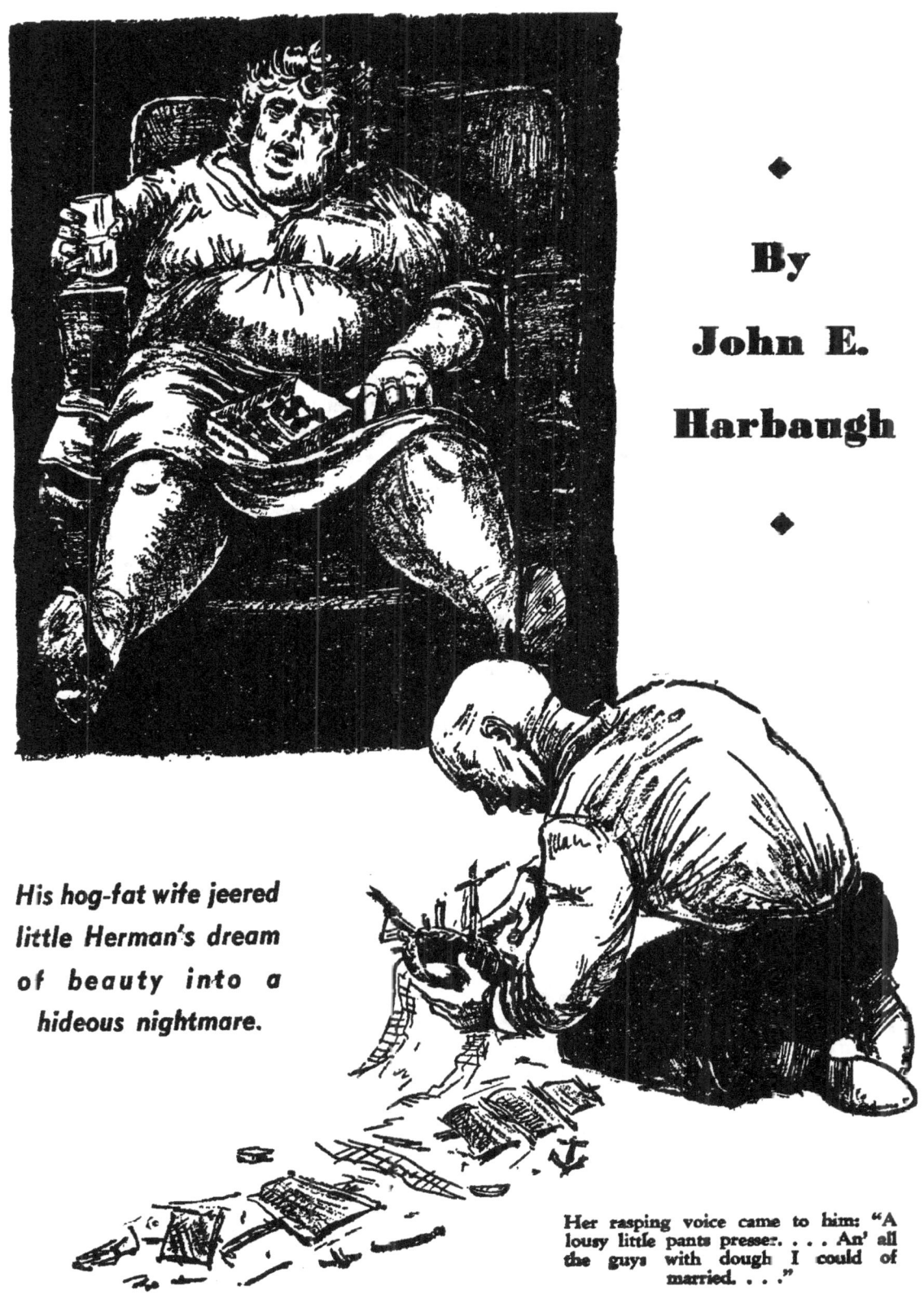

By

John E.

Harbaugh

His hog-fat wife jeered little Herman's dream of beauty into a hideous nightmare.

Her rasping voice came to him: "A lousy little pants presser. . . . An' all the guys with dough I could of married. . . ."

meals. It seeped into the very walls. Each individual odor crowded its busy way into the master fetor which proclaimed the dwelling a stable for human animals.

Herman climbed the stairs and for once, he didn't mind the hall's depressing odors. He held the epaulet tightly in his hand and his eyes were shining.

He entered his flat and glanced toward the window overlooking the street. For thirteen years he had always looked first at the window to see if she was there, as if some terrible circumstance of Fate might have removed her while he was at work. She was there tonight, though, just as she had always been there for thirteen years.

The great mountain of female flesh beside the window had long ago lost its contours. It was as though someone had shoveled three hundred pounds of soft white fat into one pile and left it beside the window. The room reeked of her unwashed body. From under a mass of stringy hair, her little, piggish eyes regarded Herman.

HER voice was shrill, petulant: "You're late tonight. You're late every night, but tonight you're later. I seen you stop and talk to the doorman. He gave you something. What was it he gave you?"

Herman held out the gold epaulet and said, "It's for *her*—in there." He pointed to the bedroom. He noticed the empty gin bottle on the window ledge, fumbled in the paper bag under his arm, and gave his wife the bottle he had just purchased.

He took the remaining contents of the bag to the kitchen. It was stifling hot in the tiny room and he decided that he would eat his supper later. Perhaps the weather would cool off later. He walked towards the bedroom, clutching the gold epaulet.

"Don't you close that door like you did last night," Rosie snarled at him.

"I get damn lonesome sittin' in this stinkin' joint all day without nobody to talk to. I ain't goin' to sit here and talk to you through no closed door."

She watched him enter the bedroom, leaving the door open. *Lousy little pants presser* she thought, *what had she married him for?* She knew why she had married him—to get out of that damn sweatshop of a bag factory on East Thirty-Second street. In those days she had been a voluptuous woman with a fine figure. She had married Herman two weeks after she met him on the Brighton Beach express to Coney Island.

But only a year after they were married, something had happened to her. She started to grow. For thirteen years she had been growing and spreading like a gross, malignant plant, until she became so large that she could no longer leave the apartment. She was still growing, still spreading, getting bigger all the time.

She lived religiously on gin and cheap chocolate candy, and hadn't had a regular meal in ten years. Her only interest in life was to sit by the window and watch the activity within the rooms of the towering hotel across the street. She knew everything that had happened in that hotel for thirteen years and planned that if she ever got her old voluptuous shape back, she would get rid of the lousy little pants-presser and get herself a guy with dough. She liked what went on in that hotel. That's where she was going to live if she ever got her shape back.

The bedroom was dark when Herman entered. It had one grimy window opening on the air-shaft, but in sixty years no occupant of the flat had ever been able to pry it open. Herman hesitated a moment. He wanted to feel just right when he looked at *her*. Then he snapped on the light switch.

In the center of the room was a scarred work table. On the table stood a ship. It was a replica of a graceful, old-time sailing ship, a detailed, scale model of the United States frigate *Congress*. Thirteen years ago, Herman had found her plans in an old naval book he had picked up in a second hand shop. For thirteen years he had labored to build her and now she was finished. That is, she was almost finished.

He sat down on the stool and placed the gold epaulet on the table. He carefully separated the strands from the shoulder board and laid them in orderly rows. Then he opened a bottle of clear cement and began to work. As he worked, the steady familiar monotone came through the open door.

"Sittin' here all the time . . . all the guys with dough I could of married . . . look at them swells goin' in the hotel . . . a lousy little pants presser . . . stuck in a joint like this . . . wastin' your life over a lousy hunk of wood . . . never gettin' nowhere. . . ."

The droning, petulant voice reached Herman's ears but he did not hear it. He hummed softly to himself as he worked. The hours slipped by and finally there were no gold strands left on the table. He stood up and walked around the work table, inspecting his little ship critically. Then he slapped the sides of his trousers in delight. The *Congress* was finished. Finished. He knew the minute he had seen the epaulets on Mr. Streech's shoulders that those gold strands were the answer.

Waves of pure rapture swept over him as he studied the model. The strands of Mr. Streech's epaulet were now worked into an intricate gold scrollwork around the stern cabins, the quarter coaches, and the trailboards. Herman suddenly realized that he was hungry, but he couldn't leave, couldn't tear his eyes from the table. The little ship stood in regal dignity, gleaming with paint and varnish and gold. She was lovely, graceful.

Finally, he sighed and went to the kitchen to eat his supper. Rosie immediately pounced upon him.

"At last you're goin' to eat," she shrilled. "Four hours you been workin' on that hunk of wood, leaving me to sit here alone. Never no regard for me or my feelin's. If Myron was here, things would be different. If Myron—"

Herman stopped suddenly and his pale little face became even whiter. "Rosie, please. Don't talk about Myron."

"Don't talk about Myron," mimicked his wife. "And why don't talk about Myron? Because *you* don't want to talk about him. Because *you* sent him where he is. It's your fault that Myron—"

Herman went into the kitchen and slammed the door. Rosie stared with unbelieving eyes. He had never dared do that before! That lousy little pants

(Please continue on page 96)

Her Black Wings

By John D. MacDonald

Three men had loved her—and died violently. . . .
◆ *I was the next target — for a malignant, phantom* ◆
boy-friend.

I STOOD with the rest of them down in the chattering damp of the 34th Street stop waiting for the express to roll in. I was on my way up to Columbia to find out if they had found room to wedge me into the graduate school. The twin lights showed in the distance and the crowd shifted a little, trying to outguess the subway system and pick a spot where the door would stop.

He didn't yell. I saw him go over the edge, half turning, his mouth wide open and silent, his fingers working fast on the empty air. His shoulders looked square and solid under the brown gabardine. They weren't solid enough. He hit the rails a split second before the steel wheels of the express ground him to blood and paste.

The crowd made exactly the same noise you hear when a touchdown play is called back for offside. A mingled groan and scream, with elements of nausea. A round little woman beside me grabbed herself by the throat and made strangled noises.

The express jammed brakes so hard that I saw the customers inside making impromptu staggering runs toward the front end. It was a waste of brakes. The boy in the gabardine had hit with his head overlapping the far rail.

They gathered around as if it was a prime dogfight. I backed out of the press, folded my paper and shoved it into my pocket. You know how it is when something happens like that. You want to make some stuffy and superfluous comment to your fellow citizen.

There was a girl standing next to me. She was tall, dressed in a sleek gray suit. Her pocketbook was a wardrobe trunk for the Singer midgets. Her black hair came down lush and thick on one shoulder. She had that city anemic look —cheekbones pushing against the pale flesh; a thin, patrician nose. Not the lips. Full of life and vitality. Her eyes were gray with a strange unfocused look.

"On the nasty side," I said to her.

She didn't answer. She didn't even look at me. I glanced down at her and saw that she held her left wrist with the fingers of her right hand. She had sunk her long dark fingernails into the flesh of her left wrist. Blood ran around the curve of her white wrist and up her arm.

"Hey!" I said. "You're hurting yourself!"

She fastened those blank gray eyes on me and murmured, "I told him he would die. I told him."

Obviously she knew the citizen who'd taken the dry dive. I glanced around. Nobody was looking at us. The cops would be along soon. The tabloids would make a tasty dish out of the situation—a dish that people riding other trains would lick their chops over. She didn't even know that I existed. I took my clean handkerchief, lifted her fingernails out of her flesh, tied the handkerchief around the four little bleeding holes. I took her

When the tide is right, a body will go out to sea. . . .

arm, turned her around, headed her toward the turnstiles and gave her a little push. She walked ahead of me quietly enough. We came up the stairs out into the sun just as a white squad car came screaming up.

She stopped when she hit the sidewalk and I steered her down the street toward the Stanlet Hotel. She stood quietly in the drugstore off the lobby while I put a dab of iodine on each hole and taped the bandage across her wrist. The gray eyes were still looking at something far in the distance.

In the bar she sat across the small table from me and looked blankly down at the straight whiskey I had bought for her. "Drink it down," I ordered.

She lifted it calmly and drank it. The harsh fingers of the liquor tightened on

33

her throat. She gasped and the tears ran down her cheeks. The glaze went out of her gray eyes. She looked at me for the first time and came apart at the seams. Fortunately we were in a dark corner of the bar. I moved over onto the bench beside her and held her fingers tightly, murmuring a lot of nothing to her until the hysteria went out of her quiet sobbing and the real tears came.

I moved back to my chair and sipped my drink, grinned at her. "Okay now?"

"I—I guess so. How did I get here?"

"You came with me. You were with the man who fell in front of the train. I thought the reporters would figure you as good material for a lush spread. I didn't think you'd like that. That bandage on your wrist is from where you gouged yourself with your fingernails."

"Who are you?" she asked, trying to smile.

"Joe Brayton. And you?"

"Judith Dikes."

"Hi, Judy."

"Hello, Joe."

"Who was the guy? Husband?"

She shuddered. "No. A friend. This was—the third time I've been out with him. His name was Ralph Lortz."

"Does anybody know you were with him?"

She frowned. "I didn't mention it to anyone. Maybe he did. He left his office to meet me. He decided that in the rush it would be easier to get uptown by subway."

"What did he do?"

"Something in investments. His number was Capital forty-six thousand five hundred sixty-nine."

"Hold it while I phone up and check."

The girl on the other end of the line said, "Mr. Lortz has left for the day. Can I take a message? No, I don't know where he would be. He didn't say. No, I don't know who he might be with. You're welcome, sir."

I went back to the table. "You're clear, Judy."

SHE WAS nice to be with and easy to talk to. Every time she remembered Lortz the little gray ghosts came back into her eyes and that rich mouth of hers trembled. I was a boy scout on a mission. I was taking her mind off the tragedy. I was being gay. The laughing young man. Full of jokes and light patter. We drank at the bar, dinnered in the Village, eveninged on 56th.

She drank steadily and too much and I couldn't tell if it was a regular habit or the result of what had happened to her down in the cool darkness of the subway cavern. But she didn't show it. At two in the morning we were at a small uptown bar. I had run out of patter and she had begun to look like the nicest thing that had ever happened to me. I put all my hopes in my eyes and looked across at her.

"You're nice, Joe," she said. "Pick up your marbles and run, Joe. Run like hell."

"What do you mean, Judy?"

"I mean run—while there's time."

"I don't get it."

Her eyes narrowed and suddenly she wasn't pretty at all. "Joe, Ralph Lortz was the third one in two months. The third. Bill Graff fell in front of a taxi. Stanley McQuade fell out of his apartment window. Get away from me, Joe. I like you. You don't want to be the next one, Joe. Do you?" She laughed and the sound of it was like small, sharp white teeth nibbling at my spinal cord.

She flew into a hundred little bits. I got her into a taxi and managed to understand the address she gave. Her teeth were chattering and she shuddered all over.

It was a walk-up apartment on 97th, a block and a half from the river. She leaned against the wall with her face in her hands while I dug in her purse for the key. I got the door open and found the lights. She took five running steps into the room and pitched herself out on her face. I shut the door, picked her up, put her on the couch, got a towel and cold water from the kitchen and swabbed her face until her eyelids fluttered and she looked up at me.

"Go away, Joe," she said faintly. "Go far away. Don't ever come back, Joe."

In a matter of minutes she was asleep. I pulled her shoes off and her suitcoat. I got blankets out of her bedroom and covered her up, tucking her in. When I'd dimmed the lights, I walked to the window, looking down at the empty expanse of 97th Street.

She had told me to go away. That was the last thing I would do. I put her key on a table and left. The door locked behind me. I walked toward the stairs. Light came from under a door near the head of the stairs.

It swung open and a man was silhouetted against the light. He said, "I was giving you five minutes more, friend. If you weren't out of there then, I was coming in after you."

"That would have been interesting," I said.

I caught a whiff of his breath as he threw a big fist at me. I stepped inside the clumsy swing and brought one up through the middle. It was harder than I wanted it to be and it hurt the hell out of my hand. But it made me look good. He went back into the room and smashed a cheap chair as he fell on it. I followed him closely and when he staggered up, I put a hand on his thick chest and shoved him back toward the bed. He sat down.

As he tried to get up I stood over him with the right hand cocked. "Better keep sitting, laddie," I said. He relaxed. He had a florid face, unkempt hair, a soiled blue shirt open at the neck and puffy eyes. I moved back and kicked his door shut.

He took the cigarette I offered him and held still for the match. His one room apartment was as neat and sweet as the inside of a hobo's shoe.

I pulled a chair around and straddled it, my forearms resting on the back of it. "Now, laddie, suppose you tell me what you expected to gain by bashing me one out there in the hall."

He mumbled, "I don't like wise guys."

"Nobody does. I didn't know I qualified. Are you a self-appointed guard for the little lady?"

"What the hell is it to you?"

"I'd be happy to hit you again, laddie."

"It's none of your business—but she lives off me, friend."

I felt sick in the middle. She'd seemed so right, somehow. "You ought to keep her home nights then," I said.

He scowled. "It isn't what you think. I've got no claim on her like that. We're both from the same town. I'm keeping her going until she gets a job. I want to marry her."

I looked at the cluttered room. "You mean you work! And still find time to keep your place so clean?"

He said sullenly, "I make good money, I'm an industrial designer."

"So you just live next to her and keep her going and expect her to drop into your lap when the debt gets high enough."

"Put it anyway you want to."

I stared at him for a few minutes. I checked back through my memory of the faces of the people on the subway platform. I couldn't build laddie into the picture, but there had been more people there than I'd had time to look at. It might just fit. If laddie had taken care of Lortz, he might have practiced on Graff and McQuade.

"What's your name?" I asked.

"Michael Burns. What's it to you?"

"Where were you today at four-fifteen?"

"I was right here. I had my day off."

He had powerful hands. Hands that

could have shoved Lortz off the edge of the platform. He sat too still. I didn't like the look of him. There was nothing to go on. If Judy had suspected him, she would have mentioned it when she told me to leave her.

"I'm Ralph Lortz," I said quietly.

He looked at me steadily. "You pack a hell of a good punch for a ghost, Lortz."

"How do you know Lortz is dead?" I asked quickly.

He waved a big hand at the radio. "Seven o'clock news." He smiled. She has a rough time with her boys friends, doesn't she?" It wasn't a pretty smile.

I fell asleep two minutes after I climbed into bed, but awakened a half hour later. Michael Burns, three times life size, was straddling the front car on a subway train, bearing down on me. I was tied hand and foot and stretched across the tracks. Burns was smiling. We weren't down in the underground, but out on a flat expanse of Daliesque desert. Judy was on her face in the sand ten feet away. I was screaming at her to untie me, but the train was making too much noise. . .

Clicking on the light, I sat on the edge of the bed and sucked a cigarette like a little kid with a straw in somebody else's soda. My hands shook and the breeze from my open window chilled the perspiration on my back.

Right then and there I decided that I'd better arrange to be number four in Burns' hit parade. That was the way out for Judy. It would either prove that all the others had been accident, or that Burns was little boy grue.

THE next afternoon was warm and Judy and I walked in the park. In the side pocket of my jacket was the comfortable weight of the little Spanish automatic I had won in a crap game in Paris. I had decided that if I told her my suspicions about Burns, she might spoil my play. It had to work right. The only way it could

work properly was by being on my toes all the time.

It was tough work to take my eyes off Judy every few minutes and take a look around. There was color in her cheeks and her lips were made for laughing. Once when we got behind a stack of shrubbery, I pulled her close and kissed her. She was laughing at the time, but after the kiss she stood close to me and I looked down into her eyes and everything was very solemn between us—like a chord of organ music you overhear as you walk by a church.

"You better not see me again, Joe," she said. "I'm bad luck."

"It's too late, now. Isn't it?" I said softly.

She didn't answer. She nodded her head quickly and lifted her face to be kissed again. It would always and forever be too late to ever leave her.

May in the month to be in love in Manhattan. You can be in love almost any month anywhere else, but it's good to save it until May when you're in the big town. We went everyplace that people go and did everything that people do and there was nobody in Manhattan except the two of us.

All except Burns. Burns was the quick look I gave behind us whenever we approached a curb. Burns was a light shining under a door after I took her home. Burns was the fear that kept me from taking a subway.

He was always around the corner from us. When I glanced behind us and saw the empty sidewalk, I knew that he had just stepped into a doorway. Always I remembered his smile.

I tried to make plans for us, but Judy always steered me away, saying, "Oh, Joe. Don't be dull. We've got a million tomorrows with sunshine every day."

It looked as though she was right.

During the first week of June she began to be jittery. She wouldn't tell me why.

Her cheeks were gaunt. On a warm night she said, "Joe, let's go back to the park. Let's go back to the place where you kissed me the first time. Please, Joe."

In the cab she clung to my arm and her eyes were bright. There was a bench near the place where I had kissed her. It was near a sharp curve in the path. She pulled me over to the bench and we sat down, side by side. She was on my right side. A cool breeze came along and she shivered. She slipped her hand down into my jacket pocket, said, "What on earth have you got in that pocket, Joe?"

I took it out. A distant light glimmered on the blued steel. "It's a gun, darling. I won it in a crap game during the war."

"Do you always carry it?"

"Yes."

"But why?"

"I like to have it around, darling."

"Is it loaded?"

"Sure. It's got a shell in the chamber. This little thing here is the safety. All you have to do is push that down and pull the trigger."

She shivered. "It frightens me. How do you hold it?"

"Like so. You've got to be careful not to get your hand too high on the grip."

"Let me hold it, Joe."

I handed it to her. She was awkward with it. I could just see her face in the dim light. She slid away from me, turned toward me and scowled with mock fury.

"Grrr! I'm going to kill you, Joe."

The look of the gun in her hand was an absurdity. I laughed. Then I heard the faint bitter sound of the safety. The scowl had faded. Her eyes were far away.

I slapped the gun with my right hand. The flare burned my wrist and a brilliant slash of pain creased my arm. She swung the gun back, and I grunted as I hit her in the face with my left fist. She crumpled and slid off the bench.

I stood up and walked blindly off into the darkness. You do silly things when the hinges come loose and your life slides down into a pile of rubble. I must have walked a hundred yards, my lips moving but making no sound. I turned and came back. She was gone. . . .

Lieutenant Weber called me up yesterday and I hurried down to Headquarters.

I sat across from him and he tapped on the desk top with his yellow pencil for a few seconds. With a violence that startled me, he smacked his palm down on a heavy manila file folder on his desk. "I'm considering this case closed, Brayton."

"How—?" I gasped.

"I admit that I took you at face value when you came in. I put some of my best men on it. They reviewed the investigations of the deaths of Graff, McQuade and Lortz. There is no proof that this Judith Dikes even knew Graff and McQuade.

(Please continue on page 98)

Skuldugger's Loot

Human skulls grinned mockingly in the merchant's window—yet thick-skulled Dutch wanted in.

After a while, a tall, shabby old gee stands in the doorway.

THIS is about Dutch Schollmer and another guy. About knives and caterpillar hairs and some other things. And about why I don't like skulls.

When I got into Brophy's Bar that morning, Brophy says that Dutch Schollmer is looking for me. He says Dutch has been hanging around since opening time, waiting for me to show. Brophy asks,

♦ ♦ ♦

By H. C. Malcolm

"What'll you have to drink, Doc?"

I say I will have beer. When it comes, I carry it into the back room. Dutch is there, battling a bottle of Brophy's bonded ant poisoning and grinning all over his face. That is is quite a job. There is a rumour that Dutch's face got so flat by pushing it against jewelers' plate glass windows so he can case the rocks on the inside. That is not so. If Dutch pushes anything against a jeweler's window—it is a brick.

He waves me into a chair and grins even more so I can admire the three gold choppers set in the middle of his upper jaw. He says, "I got us a job."

I shake my head at that. "You got a line," I tell him. "I got a line. I am a merchant. I sell things. I do not go out at night and dip my pinkies into tills. That is illegal."

He makes an impolite sound with his mouth. "So shoving paste rocks for real ain't illegal? Since when? Besides, who says you got to lift anything? You listen while I tell you."

I listen while he tells me.

It seems that the day before Dutch is down looking over some warehouses and maybe a loft or two. "Just in case," he says. "Business ain't been so good." Anyway, he runs into this little shop on Cherry Street. Being interested, he goes in.

"A joint," says Dutch, taking another hefty swing at Brophy's Best Bonded. "Only I get to shooting the wind with the old gee that runs it. And what do you think?"

I do not know what to think. Dutch runs up his lip like a burleycue curtain, flashing those gold teeth again. "Jewels. Hundreds of 'em. Old stuff. Stickers with real rubies in the handles. All kinds of rings and things. He keeps them in a safe." Dutch makes that impolite noise again. "Safe! It's more like an iron cheese box."

I finish my beer and pour some of the bonded into my glass. "He tells you they're all the real mee-mookus."

"He does."

"He feeds you a line," I say. "He probably buys it from Woolworth."

"You find out," says Dutch. He sits back and grins at me.

"I find out?"

"You case the stuff. Rocks is your business. You know the phonies. If this gee has a load of the McCoy, you tip me and I'll knock off the joint. We split forty-sixty."

"Fifty-fifty."

We argue. We settle for fifty-fifty. He gives me the address and I go to take a look.

Cherry Street isn't much of a street. It's one block long, turning off Webster. It ends against the brick side of a warehouse. There are various things in the gutter.

The shop isn't much, either. I see a hole in a wall with only one show window. The window is dirty. Over the door is a sign that says: *M. Walker, Curios.* A lot of rain water has gone over it since it was hung. I look in the window.

Except for the skulls, there isn't anything to see. There are eight skulls, set in a line. They stare at me and I stare back.

AFTER a while, a tall, shabby old gee comes out of the shop and stands in the doorway. He bows and simpers in my direction, all the time dry-washing his hands.

"You are interested in my skulls?"

I shrug my shoulders. I say not particularly. I say a friend of mine tells me he sees some very nice things in this shop.

"A friend?" I catch something happening back of the old buzzard's eyes, something unpleasant. It is gone before I decide what it means. He waves a scaly claw at the skulls. "These are purely for show. They attract attention. Won't you step inside?"

I step inside.

The shop smells of dust and other bad things. It is filled with all kinds of junk. There is junk on the tables and on the floor and on all the shelves. It is spread evenly with a layer of dust, like dirty butter on moldy bread. This character says, "My name is Walker. Now, if you'll tell me what it is you want?"

"Maybe," I say, "I got the wrong place." I wave at the stacks of stuff. "I don't see anything—"

This Walker chuckles. It is a dry sound, like loaded dice in a leather cup. "Of course not, my dear sir." He leans closer. His breath smells like Tuesday's milk on Friday. "Burglars," he whispers. "I must be careful, you know. This way, please."

He leads the way through a door. The second room is even smaller and stuffier than the first. But it is filled with different kinds of stuff. I see a lot of swords and knives and funny-looking rods. Walker takes a nasty, four-foot slicer from the wall and hands it to me. "A British naval cutlass. Is it not beautiful?"

I run a finger along the business edge. It is sharp. I say, "It is sharp."

"Of course. It would be quite useless, otherwise."

I give it back to him. For some reason, I have trouble swallowing. He does not notice. He has scuttled away and is hunching his frame over a big iron box. Over one shoulder he says, "I keep my real treasure in here. They are not for sale, you understand. I collect them."

"Collect them?"

If there is an answer to that, I miss it. He is coming back to me, carrying something in his fingers. It is a ring, a big gold ring with a lot of fancy work. "Watch," he says. He presses a spring or something. A little needle jumps out

from the center of the ring. Me, I jump too. Walker chuckles. "Clever, eh? You put poison inside. Very effective."

I say, "I think I got to go, now."

I do not get away from him, though, because he shoots out a long arm and gloms onto my elbow. "Not yet, my dear sir. I have more to show you."

He goes back to the safe, and this time he brings a leather bag. I dump it upside down over a table. The stuff that rolls out makes my eyes bulge. There are rings, pins, chokers. And the stones are as good as Uncle Sam's long green. I paw them like a kid pawing a sack of candy.

Walker isn't paying much attention. He leans over and breathes on my neck. "My friend," he says, "have you ever considered murder?"

I have a feeling under my shirt like ants crawling. I lick my lips, which are very dry. "Murder?"

"It is a hobby of mine."

"Murder?" I squeak.

He giggles very unpleasantly. "Shall we say, rather, the contemplation of murder."

I say he can if he wants. I say it is all the same to me. I look at my watch. I find it is late. I say I must go. I start to go.

HE GRABS me by the elbow again. His voice is husky and deep, like he is talking from down in a hole— A grave maybe. . . . "In ancient days," he tells me, "murder was a fine art. A knife—" he waves at the assorted pig-stickers on the walls—"a potion in a cup . . . a bit of powder, perhaps. Or caterpillar hairs."

"Caterpillar hairs?"

"The fuzzy kind. They are not used much anymore." He shakes his head sadly. "Murder isn't what it used to be. People use guns and things. No imagination."

I say, "I got a fine imagination. Too

good. And now I have to leave here."

He doesn't seem to hear me. "Very sad. Very sad." He points at the rings and stuff scattered on the table. "Did it ever occur to you what an excellent motive those things would make for murder?"

I say there are a lot of things occurring to me.

"You know, my friend, I like you. You have an interesting—" He studies my head, like a bug collector casing a prize bug. "—face. I am going to tell you something. Do you know the key to murder?"

I do not. I say the matter has never seemed very important. I say I do not really care. Walker has gone to the safe. He comes back with a big, flat, wooden box. He hisses, "This is for disposing of the body."

He opens the case. I look inside. It is filled with sawbones' tools, big ones and little ones, the kind they use to cut people open. I leave then.

When I get out into the street, I run.

Dutch is waiting for me at Brophy's. He has ruined the first bottle and is working on a second. He flashes the three gold posts when he sees me. "Well," he says, "is it the McCoy?"

I tell him it is the McCoy.

"Swell." He pours a drink and tips it down. I also pour a drink. I pour two drinks. After that, I pour two more. Dutch is rubbing his hands together. "So I crack it. Tonight I crack it wide open."

I say, when I can talk, "Leave me out."

He stares at me. "What gives, Doc? We split. You did your business. Now I do mine. We split."

I says, "I do not want any part of this deal. You don't either. I have talked to this Walker. He is not right in the head. There is something missing when they put him together. He collect skulls—personally."

Dutch only laughs. "So what? He's nuts. You think I can't handle a dried-up old member like that?"

"Okay," I say. "You handle him. Only leave me out."

"But Doc—"

"Out," I say, very firm. "All the way out."

It is nearly a week before I am in Brophy's again. I ask around for Dutch. Brophy shakes his head. "Ain't seen him for six, seven days, Doc. Ain't seen him since that time he was looking for you."

"Got thrown in the pokey, maybe," I say—kind of hopeful.

"It ain't that. I would've heard if he was. It's just he ain't around. Nobody's seen him for maybe a week."

I order a rye. Something is running around inside my head, like rats in a cellar. I order another rye, a double one. After I drink it, I go for a walk. I go over to Cherry Street.

It has not changed. There are still things in the gutter. There is still a row of skulls. I count them. There are nine.

I think: *Before there were eight.* The one on the far end is shinier than the rest, like maybe it isn't quite dry. I am sick in the gutter. As I am straightening up, painful-like, I hear a tapping on the window. I turn to look. There is a little card stuck in front of the new skull. It says: *Under New Management.*

Above it, grinning and bobbing his head and showing his three gold teeth, is Dutch.

Hell's Belle

Crime-Reporter Ben Harlow despised himself for helping exotic Roxy collect grisly murder mementos—yet he went all out to win her love with a token of funereal glamour.

He yelled: "Throw that damned thing away!"

CHAPTER ONE

Macabre Prize

IT WAS about eight o'clock that night that Ben Harlow got half drunk and started to fight that gnawing, vicious yen to see Roxy. If he'd stayed sober, he'd have left her alone and none of this would

By Robert Turner

Suspenseful Novelette of
the Devil's Own Daughter

have happened. When he was sober, he couldn't even stand the thought of Roxy Breen. When he was blanko, a condition into which he usually rushed himself full tilt—to avoid this dangerous twilight state —Roxy didn't bother him. He just didn't think about her, or about anything.

But something went wrong this night. The fifth of bourbon he'd downed as fast as he could pour it into himself had not hit bottom. It had just put an edge on him and set him on fire inside. It got him restless and irritable and started him to thinking about Roxy. Then came the terrible ache to see her.

At eight thirty the mesmeric, unearthly call could not be denied. He cabbed over to her place.

Ben Harlow got out of the hack in front of the place where she lived, a neat and flashy new apartment building that reared haughtily out of the squalor of the East Side tenement district. He stood there for a moment, sucking in deeply the last breaths of air that would seem clean and sweet to him that night.

He was a strange looking man, Harlow. He didn't look like one of the cleverest, most highly paid newspapermen in the city. He didn't look like a man that a lot of women went for and hard. He was average height, compactly built. He wore no hat and his brown hair would have had a little curl to it, if it wasn't so thin and short cropped. His extremely high, bony forehead was veined on one side. His eyes were deep into his face, with a flat, cold look to them. His face was skull-like with prominent cheek bones, and a sullen mouth that now was drawn and tight.

A fit of shivering took him, standing there, and yet he felt flushed and warm at the same time. Every nerve in him was screaming. It was always that way with him, when he got this strange, wild yen to see Roxy. He wondered vaguely what kind of a welcome he was going to get from her tonight. He had nothing for her,

no ghastly, macabre little souvenir of some bloody crime of violence. He had not brought her any for a long time, now, either. So she would probably kick him out on his ear.

But the hell with it, he told himself, he could try. Maybe it would be different tonight. Maybe she would like him for himself alone and not for some horrid little memento of a murder that he had stolen for her. But he doubted it. Roxy was like a woman made of ice when he didn't bring her anything. When he did— Perspiration began to break out on him.

He jammed his hands into the pockets of the topcoat and went in through the small flashy, chrome and leather lobby, up the elevator to the seventh floor. He knocked on Roxy's door, holding his breath tight in his throat, his nails digging into his palms.

She came to the door almost immediately. The breath burst from his throat. He felt pleasantly dizzy and full of clouds in the head, looking at her.

Roxy Breen was tall for a girl, as tall as he, in the spike-heeled, sateen slippers she wore, with the top strap high around her slender ankle. There was no classic perfection of features. Her mouth was too broad and on any other woman would have been ugly. Her green eyes were too widely set apart. And that mouth, with the full lips that were always red and wet looking, twisted at one corner in a strangely enigmatic smile, was infinitely alluring. The eyes, heavy-lidded and long-lashed, grew smoky and smouldering with a challenging look that would drive a man mad. Her hair was thick and soft-waved, a tawny blonde-brown color and it fell full around her shoulders in a long bob. It was full of highlights and alive looking, and you could hardly keep your fingers out of it.

That was the way Roxy looked to Harlow whenever he had brought her another little knicknack for her collection of weird souvenirs intimately associated with the crime of murder. That was the way she looked tonight—and Harlow felt a stab of fear. When he disappointed her, when she found out he had not brought her anything, she'd freeze up and that oddly lovely face would become a cold, hard mask. She'd abuse him and kick him out.

HIS eyes moved over her and he had to moisten his lips, they were so hot and dry. She was wearing a set of Chinese-red lounging pajamas. The tasseled belt was tight about her wisp of waist. In one slender-fingered hand, with carmined nails long and sharp as claws, she carelessly held a cigarette. Smoke streamed up from it in a thin, straight line until it hit her face and then broke around it.

"Ben!" she said. She had a deep and throaty voice. The wet-looking lips broke to show sharp and shiny little teeth. "Ben, I was praying you would come tonight. I was going crazy to see you."

She didn't reach to his pocket like she always did, to see if he had anything for her. That was strange. She stepped aside and he went past her, the heavy, oriental perfume she wore catching his nostrils for an instant, with a peculiar, opiate-like effect.

He walked the foyer, thick with expensive carpeting, and came out into a large, studio-type living room. It hit him like it always did—as if he were suddenly drugged, and all kinds of weird and exotic impulses seized him.

It was a strange room. It was close and almost hothouse warm, with the mingled scents of turkish tobacco, a touch of incense and that heavy, mucky perfume of Roxy's. The furniture was oddly assorted. There was a lot of teakwood and ebony. The chairs and sofa were all oversized and littered with silken pillows. There were mirrors everywhere, most of them colored. On a cocktail table was a newly opened fifth of expensive bourbon, as though Roxy had been expecting him, or

thinking of him—because she drank bourbon only with him. Ordinarily, her taste ran to fancy liqueurs.

But the thing that always caught Harlow's eye, was the shelf, over the sofa, just at arm's reach from it. He didn't want to look at it, but it always drew his eyes with an unholy fascination.

It was Roxy's shelf of souvenirs; a strange and horrible assortment of articles connected with violent deaths. There was a piece of a broken vial that had held poison with which a man had murdered his family. There was an inch-long piece of wire, part of the garrot a notorious strangler had used. There was a ragged piece of wall paper, stained brown with dried blood. And an upholsterer's awl, that had been plunged through the throat of a blonde model. Dozens of similar items were arranged neatly on that shelf, each a gruesome relic of some particularly horrendous homicide.

On the wall, over this shelf, were hung a few choice larger items that were Roxy's pride and joy. A jagged hunk of rusty metal that had been part of a spade used to dig a lonely grave for a maniac's victim. A stump of polished wood, the handle of the instrument of death in a series of bloody axe murders. A piece of insulated wire that had supplied the current for the electric chair in the death house. The finger of a rubber glove which had been worn by a famous surgeon who had gone berserk and reverted to the days of his early youth when he had been a butcher's assistant.

As Ben Harlow's bleak eyes wandered over all these macabre mementos, he remembered the first time he'd seen them. At the time, the significance of them had not penetrated. Laughing almost childishly, Roxy had told him that it was just a hobby with her, that she was just "another collector." She merely collected little souvenirs connected with the crime of murder. Like someone else would collect matchbook covers or odd buttons, or coins or stamps.

It was not long before Harlow realized that was not so. It was more than a hobby with Roxy, this strange collection. They held a special significance and association of ideas for her. It was an almost fiendish fetish. She worshiped those murder mementos. She would fondle them with the same delighted concentration of a child playing with its toys.

It was not until after Roxy had gotten her strange, unearthly hold on him, had gotten into his system like the virus of some dread disease, that Harlow had learned the truth about her. And then it was too late for him to do anything about it.

From the first moment she had met him, learned that he was a newspaper man, Roxy had cultivated him, had gone out of her way to please him. And when Roxy Breen sought to please a man, the *femme fatales* of history were put to shame. It was easy, after that, to get him to help her add to the collection.

He'd tried to fight it, at first. But being the crime reporter for the *Globe*, Harlow was in the middle of every big murder in the city. And every time he came upon a crime scene, he would find himself instinctively looking around for some choice little item that he might be able to sneak out and take to Roxy; something that would especially please her. To get them, he had taken considerable risk of getting into serious trouble with the police authorities.

While he was standing there, staring at Roxy's bizarre collection, he felt a light touch on his sleeve. He turned slowly. Roxy was standing behind him, holding out a water tumbler, half full of golden bourbon.

"You look bad, lover," she said, with her head cocked to one side a little, looking up at him from under her thick lashes and dark and shiny eyelids. Her voice was almost a hoarse, insinuating whisper. "You need a drink."

HE REACHED out and took the glass, watching the trembling of his own hand. He downed the liquor fast, feeling the pleasant burn of it, all the way down his gullet. It quieted the wings of the butterflies in his stomach. He set the glass down.

"Come here, baby!" he husked.

She glided toward him, with a sort of rhythmic, liquid grace of motion. His eyes clung to her face as she came very close to him. He looked at the half-parted, moist redness of her lips, with the thin white shine of teeth between them. Her nostrils were flared. Her smoky green eyes were beginning to take on that sort of wild, ecstatic glitter that he knew so well. He didn't understand it because this was the way Roxy was when he brought her another murder souvenir—and only then. Yet, tonight, he had brought her nothing.

He didn't question this miracle, though. He accepted it gratefully and reached out and hungrily pulled her close. She leaned back from the waist, her head thrown back, so that her long hair hung loosely. Her eyes closed almost completely. He looked down at the tight, clean arch of her white throat with a tiny pulse beating madly at the side of it.

"You're a beautiful woman, Rox!" he breathed.

A touch of teasing smile flirted about her mouth. She put her pale, graceful hands flat on his chest. "You love me very much, Ben?"

"What do you think?" he answered, his voice catching. It was the answer he always gave her. Because he didn't love her. He hated her—and feared the insidious hold she had upon him. Yet his arm tightened around her waist.

She raised her head and her eyes looked straight into his, pleadingly. "Ben, you—you've got to do something for me."

"Sure," he heard himself saying.

She had made a little childish chuckling sound of delight back in her throat, and then began to speak quickly, breathlessly: "There's a girl lives in the next apartment, Ben. A young girl, quite beautiful. You know how thin the walls are, here. Well—Ben, something happened there next door, tonight."

"Happened? . . . What do you mean, Rox?"

Her lips pulled back from her teeth and the pupils of her eyes seemed to shrink and pinpoint. "Somebody killed her, Ben. Right next door, there. I heard it. I heard them quarreling, a man's voice cursing her. Then there was the sound of a struggle and the muffled report of a shot. . . . Right next door, Ben!"

It took a moment for it to penetrate. Then he grabbed her by the arms, cruelly, feeling his fingers bite into the soft round flesh. "What are you getting at, Rox?" He *knew*, though. He didn't really have to ask.

"I didn't call the police, Ben. I—I've been trying to work up nerve to go over there myself. But I couldn't quite make it. But *you'll* go for me—won't you, Ben?"

He shook her, but the weird and strangely exciting look of rapture and anticipation stayed set on her face. He couldn't shake it away. "You're out of your mind!" he told her. "You're mad!" He flung her away from him.

He walked over and stood by the window, looking out at the turgid, slow moving blackness of the East River, a few blocks away. His heart was hammering wildly. He felt like he was suffocating. He said: "Damn it to hell, Rox, I've done everything for you. I've risked losing my job, jail sentences, to satisfy that hellish craving of yours. But this is too much. Do you realize what you're asking me to do?"

She came over behind him and the sultry scent of her got into his nostrils. Softly, she whispered: "You won't be sorry, Ben." The sound of her voice strummed his tortured nerves like a musician's sensitive fingers on the strings of a guitar. "I'll have never had anything like that before. Something taken from the scene of a killing before even the police got there! Think what that will mean to me, Ben. . . ." Her voice trailed off.

He wheeled around suddenly, his ugly, tough face showing the strain upon it. He kept wiping the sweating palms of his hands up and down the sides of his trousers. The way she stood there now, the wildness in her eyes was more alluring then he had even seen it before. He couldn't fight the hellish, soul-destroying appeal this strange woman held for him.

"All right, damn you!" he told her.

SHE came over to him and brushed his mouth with hers teasingly. "Hurry, Ben, lover! You can get into the other flat through the connecting dumbwaiter shaft."

It was easy, once he started. With a kitchen knife, he jimmied the catch of the dumbwaiter door of the other apartment, climbed across and came out into the other kitchen. He was moving mechanically, now, like a man mesmerized; not frightened, not nervous, only emotionally numbed—with one thought in mind . . . to get something special for Roxy's collection and get back to her presence.

This kitchen was in darkness, but he could see out a door into the lighted living room. He stood there for a moment, listening, but there was so sound except the slight whir of the motor of an electric clock. Outside, on First Avenue, seeming far away and unreal, he could hear the sound of traffic.

He moved lightly out of the kitchen and into the big studio living room. The place was a shambles. Several chairs were overturned and broken. A lamp lay shattered on the floor. Another had its shade all askew but was still burning. The drawers of a desk had been yanked out and ransacked.

And then he saw the girl. Roxy had been right. She was quite beautiful. She had long, ash-blonde hair and lovely translucent skin. She was wearing a simple, black, silk jersey dress and she had the figure for it. She was lying on her side, half twisted about, so that her face was toward him. She had long, exquisitely shaped legs.

There was an ugly, dark hole in her dress, right over the breast, and a shiny wet stain had spread all around it in an intricate design. Her mouth was like a small, flaming red pennant against the ghastly pallor of her face. Her eyes were open and glazed looking and vacant.

At the last moment, just as he was about to shift his gaze from her face, he detected the faintest flickering of motion in her eyes. She was still alive. Swiftly, he kneeled beside her. "Can you speak?" he whispered.

The lips parted perceptibly, with a faint little snapping sound. He had to bend his ear down close to her mouth to hear. For several moments, he couldn't distinguish words and then he heard: ". . . please . . . the lipstick . . . before . . . get here . . . lipstick . . . in—in my purse. . . ."

He waited for more, but there wasn't any more. Those few words seemed to have exhausted her. It didn't make sense in a way. The only thing he could figure was that the girl wanted to make up a little before the police and the rest of them came. It must be some dying moment's quirk of vanity. It was not too strange. Often suicides bathed and groomed and dressed themselves up in their finest clothes before committing the act.

Swiftly, he glanced about the wrecked room and when he didn't see any sign of the girl's purse, he moved into the bedroom, flicked the wall switch. This room too had been thoroughly searched. The purse he was looking for, was on the dressing table, its contents emptied out and scattered. He picked up the lipstick, took it out to the other room.

This time when he kneeled down beside the girl on the floor and spoke to her, there was no answer. The wide open staring eyes didn't move. He reached down to the wrist of the hand flung out at her side. There was no pulse. She had gone while he was out of the room. She was dead.

He started to get up again and then remembered her pleading. He looked down at her deadly pale face and saw that her lip rouge was mostly rubbed off. She was such a pretty thing that he could understand her desire to look as lovely as possible when the strangers came to stare at her.

With his hands trembling, he quickly unscrewed the top of the lipstick tube, levered up the smooth, waxy stub of bright red paint. As gently and expertly as possible, he complied with the dead girl's dying wish. When he finished, he screwed the top of the tube back on. As he looked down at that little brass casing, a strange, unbidden excitement stirred deep inside of him.

Think what that will mean to me, Ben. . . .

His fist closed tight about the lipstick for an instant, the knuckles standing out whitely. Roxy would go crazy if she got this. It would be the greatest prize of her collection.

At the same time that he was thinking this, self-revulsion and nausea formed in him. How could he do this unspeakable thing, feed and gratify that monstrous, abnormal fetish of Roxy's?

Think what that will mean to me, Ben. . . .

Then torturing memories of the hours he'd spend in Roxy's arms, the touch of her burning mouth, the cool caress of her long fingers, filled his mind and pushed out every other emotion. He stood up stiffly and dropped the tube of lip rouge into his pocket. Quickly, he left the murder apartment the same way he had entered.

Roxy Breen was waiting for him in her own kitchen. She stood before him, her eyes watching his hand with frozen fascination as he dug into his pocket. "I've been going crazy, Ben," she breathed. "I could hardly wait. What did you bring me, Ben, lover? Show me! Show me!"

While he pulled the lipstick from his pocket, he told her about the scene in the neighboring apartment. He told her of the dying girl's request and the thing

he had done. Now, it was his turn to tantalize her. Instead of handing the lipstick tube to her, he kept it in his fist, and hid it behind his back.

She threw herself against him, reached her arms around him, her face close to his, her eyes like deep pools of swirling green liquid fire into which he seemed to be falling: "Give it to me, Ben! she pleaded in an agonized voice.

Then she kissed him, her mouth warm and clinging. While she trapped him like that, her hands, behind his back, found his. She wrenched the tube of lipstick away from him. She tore her mouth away from his and twisted clear of him, backed off. She held the lipstick cupped in both hands and looked down at it, the sound of her breathing audible. She fondled the tiny souvenir of death and cooed over it.

"Oh, Ben, Ben!" she murmured. "Look what I've got! Think of it, Ben!" Her strangely beautiful face was alight now. Her eyes were shining. Her tiny, pointed red tongue flicked swiftly across her lips. And through all this exotic loveliness shone the ghoulish hunger of her twisted, abnormal mind.

Ben Harlow whispered, a barely audible sound: "You're insane. . . ." He felt that he was going to be ill.

CHAPTER TWO

Mad Molly's Place

THE place was a Third Avenue dive, long and narrow and dark inside. It's formal name was the Newsman's Bar & Grille but to every newspaperman in Manhattan it was known merely as Mad Molly Malone's place. There was nothing much to it—a long bar and tables in the rear but the drinks were large and cheap and every fourth one was on the house. You could get drunk and not get rolled. You could run up tabs as large as you wanted, if Mad Molly knew you and liked you.

The place was empty when Ben Harlow walked in, except for Mad Molly Malone, herself, behind the bar. She was a great mountain of a woman, with frizzy bleached blonde hair and more war paint on her wrinkled, saggy-jowled face than on an Indian chief. Mad Molly had been a sob-sister in her prime. She knew newspapermen and loved them all—especially Ben Harlow.

She greeted him now, boisterously, fondly, with a choice of vocabulary that would have done a dock walloper proud. "Where you been, you baboon?" she demanded. "They had the stomach pump into you again? I ain't seen you in three days. Or else you been up in your room drinkin' all by yourself. What's the matter, you want to become an alcoholic or somethin'?"

He didn't even look at her. He hiked his lean hips up onto a bar stool and put his face into his hands. "Molly," he said, "make it bourbon and make it the biggest glass you can find in the place."

She stared at him, her fat-buried eyes narrowed shrewdly, her carmined mouth softening in a slight, sad smile. She tugged at a heavy, solid gold Gypsy ear ring that pierced the lobe of her right ear. She shook her head knowingly. "Ben," she said. "Poor, poor Ben."

She turned and fixed him a drink, only she made it a small highball glass and she only poured it half full. He ignored it for several moments until finally Molly said: "You been up to see that girl, that dam' girl. That zombie! What's her name? . . . She gives me the creeps just to look at her. She comes in here, it's like a cold, damp draft from the cellar."

He raised his head out of his hands then. You could almost see the remorse and misery and tearing of his conscience in his laxed face, for a moment, before he got control and tightened his features.

"Roxy!" he said. "That's her name." He raised the glass of bourbon in trembling fingers. "May she fry in hell!" He threw the drink down and almost gagged. He banged the glass on the bar, signaling for a refill.

While she poured him another drink, Molly Malone said. "It's none o' my dam' business I know but I got to say my piece again. I don't know whether you're dumb or just don't give a dam', but there's something wrong with that gal. I don't just mean she's a tramp, Ben. It's her eyes. They got all the wickedness in the world in them. You mark my words, you get yourself clear o' that baggage or she'll get you into trouble, Ben. Bad trouble!"

He looked at her and pursed his mouth, his eyes bleak and hard. "I know," he said.

She raised her finely penciled brows, corrugating her forehead. "You know? Then what the hell's the matter with you, Ben?"

"She gets me, Molly. She makes me hate my guts for even looking at her. But if I stay away too long, I'm a guy with the shakes, I'm like a snow-bird away from the stuff too long. She's like a part of me—an appendage or evil growth that I can't cut off and still live."

"The dam' zombie!" said Molly Malone.

"I'll drink to that." Harlow made a face and smacked his lips. He felt the numbness beginning to start in his fingers. He was going to make it tonight, after all. He was going to get drunk. He could tell. There would be that blessed blackout tonight, after all.

Two drinks later, the numbness had spread from Harlow's fingers all through his body. His face was amiably vacuous. The memory of the time he'd spent in Roxy Breen's flat and in the apartment next door to her's was fading to the back of his mind, like something that had happened a long time ago.

Meanwhile, a redheaded girl had come in and was sitting several stools down from him. Several times, he sensed that she was lookng his way, but he ignored her. The hell with her.

He had one more drink and managed to get down off the stool without falling on his face. He said: " 'Scuse me, Molly. Somethin' I got to do."

He weaved toward the telephone booth in the back of the place, squeezed inside. Slowly, he found and inserted his finger into the right holes on the dial. Then he fumbled a pencil stub into his teeth and talked around the clenched stub:

"Westbrook Arms . . . Forty-seventh near First . . . Apartment Seven A . . . Girl murdered. . . ."

He severed the connection. Just as he was easing back onto the bar stool again, he saw the redheaded girl meticulously applying lipstick. He shuddered and for a flashing moment, the fumes cleared from his brain and he saw the face of the dead blonde girl as he had painted her forever-stilled lips.

Harlow swore under his breath and went to work on the fresh drink Molly had set up. But this time his heart wasn't in it. He had trouble getting it down. He tried not to but he kept glancing at the redhead down the bar. Once again he saw her open her purse, take out a tissue, wipe her mouth and redo it again.

He knew that she was doing it for his benefit—and the knowledge made his flesh crawl.

ABOUT the fifth time she did it, he swung around on his stool to face her directly. She was taking great pains to put the lip rouge on just perfectly. Through the fog of alcohol and anger in his eyes, he took notice of what she looked like for the first time. She was a redhead all right, and not the blazing orange kind. Her hair was soft, sunset red and very sleekly coiffed to fit her small, heart-shaped face.

She had the usual fine white complexion of the redhaired. Her profile was nice, a gently tipped nose and a good, strong little chin. She was wearing a simply tailored green suit. The way she was sitting on the stool, legs crossed, one of them angling out enough to display nylon encased knee, calf and ankle, she let you form your own opinion about them.

Harlow's opinion was that he'd seen better and he'd seen a hell of a lot worse. They were sturdy legs, very well turned out.

"What do you think you're doing?" He demanded, staring at the strong, neat little hand that wielded the lipstick on her mouth.

She didn't stop, or pay any attention to him until she had finished. Then she

turned slowly and he got the full-on affect of her face. She had deep blue eyes with unplucked, natural brows above them. The eyes regarded him amusedly. Her mouth would have been small and just full enough, if it hadn't been so thick with red paint.

"If you're speaking to me," she said smiling, "I'm rouging my lips. Do you object to a woman making up her face?"

He considered that, studying her owlishly. While she waited for his answer, she picked up a martini and sipped at it, without taking her eyes off him. It was a little unnerving and she had already rattled him by the constant application of lipstick.

He got off the stool, perilously maintaining an upright position and made his way toward her. He stood close to her, his fists planted on his hips. "I object to you makin' a career out of it," he told her.

"Oh?" she arched her brows. "Maybe you don't like the way I do it? Perhaps *you'd* like to do it for me?" She flicked open her bag and pulled out a lipstick, held it toward him.

He looked down at that little metal tube and felt his stomach shrivel. He slapped her hand, knocking the lipstick out of it, clean across the room.

The redhead said: "Tch, tch! Now you'll have to buy me another."

Mad Molly yelled: "Harlow, what the hell's got into you? Leave this gal alone!"

The redhead said softly: "I'm sorry. I didn't know my little gag was really getting you. Will you forgive me—and let me buy you a drink?"

In the face of her quiet apology, some of the tension left his raw nerves. He drew himself up with ludicrous dignity.

"Thank you," he said. "Pleasure. I will."

He tried to be very casual, very formal about the thing. They had three drinks.

She was very young and there was a healthy, wholesome quality about her that he hadn't run up against in a long time. She had a quick, easy, infectious laugh and although he wasn't getting any more sober, with each drink, his black mood was lifting.

She told him that her name was Fay Conover and that she was twenty-one and worked in an office. She came from Grand Rapids. After while when she left the bar to powder her nose, Mad Molly came over. Mad Molly was grinning roguishly.

"That's better, Ben," she said. "Much better. There's a gal would do you a lot of good."

"Are you kidding? She's a sweet little kid. Why she should go getting herself loused up with me?"

"That's all right," Molly said. "She goes for you. Besides—she ain't no dam' zombie."

Mad Molly shouldn't have said that. For Ben Harlow's eyes clouded. Red-headed Fay Conover had melted that numbing wall of hate he had set up against Roxy. Ben Harlow was as tight as a tick but he was human again— and fair game for that terrible gnawing to see Roxy.

Harlow had walked out on Roxy, left her crooning over that macabre lipstick. And now, he was beginning to wonder if he hadn't been a fool.

WHEN Fay Conover came back she sensed the change in Harlow. She said: "You seem different, Ben, you haven't smiled once in ten minutes. Have another drink."

They had several drinks, but the party mood had fled. Fay slid gracefully off her stool. "I've got to go, Ben. I really *must*."

He stood up too, and was quite steady on his feet. This alarmed him more than if he had fallen flat on his face. The drinks were having no effect on him. He recognized this state, and a cold knot twisted his stomach. He took Fay's arm, saying:

"I'll take you home."

He hailed a cab. Fay gave an address to the hackie which he didn't catch. In the darkness of the cab he became conscious of the delicate scent of Fay's perfume. He decided that he liked it. And then he found himself comparing it with the cloying, musky scent of Roxy's heady perfume.

Fay Conover watched his face in the flash and shadow of passing street lights. Finally, she said: "To ignore me this way, and especially in a cab, you must be thinking of your best girl. And she must be pretty special."

Harlow's laugh was short. "She's special all right. There's no one like her on earth. I'll bet she'd even be special in hell." His voice roughened. "I'd like to cut out her black heart."

Fay stared at him in amazement.

The cab suddenly swung into the curb, ending their conversation. Harlow handed Fay out of the cab and paid the fare. Then he started toward the front door of the building.

Halfway across the sidewalk, he stopped as suddenly as though he'd bumped into a stone wall. He looked at the modernistic entranceway to the apartment, with the scrolled iron-work over the glass doors. He looked at the neat sign that said: *Westbrook Arms*. He looked at the number. It was the same. The apartment Fay Conover was taking him into was the same building that Roxy Breen lived in.

"What's the matter, Ben?" Fay asked, knitting her brows.

"Matter?" He stood there, staring at her. "You mean to tell me that you live *here?*"

"Of course." She laughed. "It's really a very nice place. Why, Ben?"

For a moment, he didn't answer her. He told himself that it was just a coincidence. It had to be. One of those things.

"Nothing," he said finally. "I had you figured for a different setup. Don't mind me, Fay. I say and do batty things."

"Which means—" she laughed and took hold of his arm— "you need a drink. Come on upstairs for a nightcap. . . . If you want to, that is."

"If I ever turned down a free drink, my ancestors would spin in their graves," he told her and went on it.

There was a tightening of his nerves as he crossed the familiar lobby, going up in the same elevator he'd used so many times, calling on Roxy. He could use a drink—a lot of them. Then his ears began to roar as he noticed the lift stop at the seventh floor. He stopped himself from saying anything. But when she halted in front of the door of 7 A, right next door to Roxy's—place the door that led into the flat where the blonde girl had been murdered—he couldn't take any more.

He caught her arm hard. "This is your apartment?" he said through his teeth. "You're certain of that?"

She faced him squarely. "Ben, what's the matter with you? You must think I'm a burglar, going around breaking into strange peoples' apartments." She fumbled a key from her purse, started to insert it into the lock.

He grabbed her arm again. "Fay, have you a roommate. a blonde girl, pretty and—"

She shook her head, frowning. "No. I live here alone. What are you getting at? You sure must need a drink. Come on."

And then Ben Harlow suddenly realized that the cops should be here. He'd called them. They investigated every call. There should have been police cars galore downstairs. The hall here should have been alive with reporters and cops.

"Honey," he said, "lead me to that drink!"

Fascinated, he watched her key the door open, step inside and flick the foyer switch. He followed her, noting that there was a light ahead of them in the living room. The door slammed shut behind him. And then he saw Fay Conover stop just inside the living room and suck in her breath noisily and fling the back of her hand against her mouth.

He rushed quickly up alongside of her, sure that she'd spotted the body. His eyes jerked to the spot on the floor where the corpse of the blonde girl had sprawled. *It was gone.* All the furniture had been righted and the broken pieces removed. There wasn't a sign of any kind of violence.

Someone said in a deeply quiet, amused voice: "Hi, folks!"

CHAPTER THREE

The Fatal Lipstick

BEN HARLOW whirled toward the sound and saw a man sitting in a chair in the far corner. He was a big man, with ruddy cheeks and little chips of blue ice where his eyes should have been. His head was bald, except for a fringe of curly blond ringlets above the ears. But for the eyes and the thin, cruel line of his mouth, he might have looked like a round-faced, jolly blond Friar. He was quietly and expensively dressed. He buffed the manicured nails of a large, soft looking hand, on the lapel of his suit.

He grinned at Harlow. He had small, close set, yellow teeth. "Hullo, Harlow, m'boy," he said. "You get around, don't you?"

"Sure I do," Harlow admitted. "But hereafter I'll be a little more choosy about where I go. This isn't a pleasure, Lieutenant Pederson, sir."

The big, baldheaded man laughed, held out his buffed nails in front of him, examined them.

Fay Conover said in a small voice: "What's going on here, Ben? What's this man doing here in my apartment?"

"This is Lieutenant of Detectives Pederson, Homicide Department," he told her. "He's probably looking for a misplaced body or something."

"Could be," Pederson admitted. He turned to the girl. "Sorry to bust into your place this way, Miss. But we got an anonymous phone call that there had been a murder committed here. It turned out to be a crank call. Nothing was wrong when we got here. We had the super let us in. But I thought I'd hang around until the tenant came back and sort of double check. You never can tell about these things."

"A—a murder?" Fay gasped. "There must be some mistake."

"Obviously," Pederson admitted. He screwed up his face wisely and stared hard at Harlow. "You know, son," he said, "it's peculiar that you showed up here."

"Why?"

"Because you're usually boiled—and you might've got the notion to play a prank on the Department. Like maybe some pranks—like swiping bits of evidence from the scene of a lot of murder cases?" His voice got steely hard. "Don't ever let me catch you at it, Harlow...."

Fay Conover said brightly: "Let's all have a drink."

"Thank you, no, Miss Martin," said the lieutenant. "Sorry to bother you. We get these crank calls all the time, but we've always afraid not to cover them."

They both watched him pick his coat and hat off the sofa, don them and lumber toward the door. He stopped at the doorway of the room and turned back to Harlow. He rubbed the ring of blond curls around his massive head. "So long, Harlow," he said. "Watch your step."

Harlow just curled his lip. Fay showed Pederson to the door. When she came back, Harlow said:

"Miss *Martin*, eh? What's the story, sister? This isn't your flat."

She moved over to the table where she'd set down her purse. She opened it with her back toward him. When she turned around, she had a small, nickel-plated pistol in one fist, pointed at his stomach. The sweet expression on her face had changed. She looked a little older, now. She looked just as pretty except that now there was a very desperate expression around her eyes and in the set of her small mouth. The chin looked very determined.

Her voice changed too as she snapped: "*I'm* going to ask the questions, you rum-dum newshound. Where it is?"

He raised his brows. "Where is *what?*"

"Look, Harlow," she said. "I know your rep. You're one of the trickiest guys in the business. But I never figured you for a dirty rotten, lowdown heel. I—I could shoot you . . . and get a medal!"

Harlow said: "Give me the drink first—then shoot."

SHE took a deep, exasperated breath, waggled the gun at him. "I want *that* lipstick," she said. "I'm going to get it from you if I have to shoot all your teeth out, one by one."

His mouth grew taut at mention of the lipstick. It brought back the memory of the dead blonde's lips. He kept stalling: "What lipstick?"

"Look," she said levelly. "I was getting off the elevator this evening and spotted you coming from this direction. I turned the other way, figuring you might have come from this apartment. Then I found Stella Martin lying dead on the floor—and the lipstick gone. I figured you were the one who got it, Harlow."

"I see," Harlow said. He didn't at all. His brain was whirling. "How did you catch up with me again?"

"That was simple. The first and most logical place to look was at Mad Molly's, the newsboys' hangout."

"So that business with the lipstick, in there, wasn't just a gag?" he said.

"No. I wanted to see what effect it would have on you. Well, I soon found out."

Harlow didn't want to talk about that, so he said: "You were here after I was. You saw the wreck the place was, you saw blonde Stella lying on the floor. And when you came back with me, you found all of that changed. Who do you figure cleaned up in here? And where is Stella's body?"

Fay Conover said: "You tell me, Harlow. . . . Turn around. You've got that lipstick and I'm going to search you and find it."

Slowly, he turned around. He heard her move up behind him. He waited until she'd dipped her hand into his side pocket, then said: "Suppose Lieutenant Pederson didn't leave but is hanging around outside—listening to all of this?"

The natural instinct would be for her to turn her head toward the door, then. Harlow counted on it, swung around and rammed down hard with his arm, across her gun wrist. She gave a little cry. He kicked the pistol across the floor away from him and twisted her arm.

She cried: "You're breaking my arm! Please! Please!"

"Hold still," he told her. "If you don't move or try to get away, it won't hurt."

While he held her with one hand, he stripped his necktie off with the other. He caught her other hand behind her back and bound her wrists hurriedly with the necktie. He turned her around to face him.

"I hate to do this, honey," he said. "But this all smells like something big to my newsy nose. I'm going to park you out of the way, while I go to work."

Fay didn't say anything, just glared at him.

Harlow prodded her toward a closet, shoved her inside and shut the door. Then he left the apartment and turned toward the one next door—where Roxy Breen lived.

He went to knock on Roxy's door, and found it ajar. He pushed the door open with the tips of his fingers. The next instant, he was running across the foyer toward the living room of Roxy's apartment. He could see her there, struggling with a dark and stocky man in overalls and work shirt. The man had Roxy by the throat and was choking her.

THE man turned when he heard Harlow's footsteps. He took his hands from Roxy's throat and she stumbled back out of the way. But the dark man was a little slow in spinning around and getting his guard up. Ben Harlow started his swing, while he was still a couple of feet away. It landed with the extra momentum full against the dark man's jaw. The dark man made a grunting noise and dropped, colder than a gaffed cod.

Harlow looked down at him. The man on the floor was heavy featured, with a prominent, bulldog jaw. His black hair, streaked with iron-gray, was short cropped. He wore a thick, untrimmed black mustache. There was a slightly foreign cast to his features.

"Who is he, Roxy?" Harlow demanded. "What was he choking you for?"

He looked up at her. She was still wearing the red lounging pajamas. Her green eyes were glowing as if she had enjoyed the violence of the few minutes. She was gently caressing the bruise marks on her throat. She spoke in low, husky tones:

"So you came back, lover boy."

Harlow pointed at the prone dark man. "Who is he?"

"He said he was the plumber of the building. He's been in here for over an hour, supposedly fixing the radiator. He noticed me examining the lipstick you brought me—from over there." She gestured vaguely toward the next apartment. "He went berserk, then. He jumped me, tried to get the lipstick away from me."

Her wet-looking mouth twisted. "*No-body is going to get that lipstick away from me, Ben. I fought him, and he tried to choke me. Then you came in."

"There's something mighty important about that lipstick," Harlow said. "Too many people want it. I'm beginning to think I got the dead girl's request all wrong. I don't think she wanted me to make her up at all. She was trying to tell me something about that lipstick. . . . Where is it, now, Rox? Let me see it for a moment."

A crafty look narrowed her green eyes. She slipped an arm around his shoulder, moved close to him. She smiled lazily and said: "Of course, lover boy. It's under the sofa. It fell on the floor during my struggle with—him." She shifted her gaze to the unconscious self-styled plumber on the floor. "I kicked it under the sofa so he wouldn't see it."

Harlow strode toward the divan, kneeled down and looked underneath it. He reached his hand as far under as he could and swept it round in a semi-circle. He said: "Are you sure, Rox? I can't find it under here, anywhere."

She said: "Can't you lover?" Her voice was soft and silky, and it suddenly occurred to him that it was very close. She was standing right over him. He started to turn his head to look up at her but he never made it. The whole world seemed to suddenly explode in a shower of fireworks. He went swimming off into thick, inky blackness. . . .

When Ben Harlow came out of it, he couldn't remember a thing. That wasn't unusual. He was used to awaking under those conditions. His head felt as though a million little pixies were holding a riot inside of it. He was certain some of them were walloping his temples with miniature sledge hammers. And that was okay, too. That wasn't out of the norm. He put his hands to his head, hoping he could hold it in place for just a few more moments.

He said to himself: "Drunk again, Harlow, you sot! And a whizbanger, this time."

One of his hands gravitated toward the back of his skull and he winced as his exploring fingers found a lump raised back there. From somewhere he gathered a lot of strength and managed to reach a sitting position. His stomach pitched. He tried to look around, but everything slanted and tipped and whirled.

But he stuck at it and pretty soon the merry-go-round stopped. His eyes opened wider and wider as he saw that he wasn't in his own little two-by-four room. He was in Roxy Breen's place.

Then it all came suddenly shooting back into his mind. He reached out and caught hold of a chair and pulled himself to his feet. He stood there, looking around. On the floor, near him, was one of Roxy's souvenirs. It was the piece of broken spade and he decided that was the weapon she had used to hit him with.

He suddenly realized that he was alone in the room. Roxy was gone. The phony plumber was gone. A dozen questions poured through his mind. He worried them around, but got nowhere.

There was suddenly a ringing sound that at first he thought came from his own battered head. After a moment, he separated it from the sounds inside his skull and tabbed it as the ringing of Roxy's telephone. Staggering a little, he walked over to the little table that held the instrument. He barked an "hello" and an operator's twanging voice told him: "I have that call to Wick Harbor for you now, sir."

He winced, started to say that he hadn't wanted any call to Wick Harbor. And then he realized that someone had wanted

that call put through, not so long ago. It must have been a man, because the operator thought it was he who had made the first call. The only other man who had been here was the fake plumber, who had wanted the mysterious lipstick badly enough to strangle Roxy. Harlow said:

"Okay. Put it through."

There was a pause and some buzzing and then a feminine voice with the most delightful French accent he'd ever heard said: " 'Ello! Zis ees ze Temple of ze Disciples of Damon. Lizette speaking."

Harlow gulped. "The temple of— *what?*"

She repeated the name and then demanded: "Who is zis?"

Harlow said confidentially: "Listen, I've got the lipstick. What do I do now?"

There was a silence from the other end. But the ruse didn't work. She laughed: "You seely man, you. What does Lizette care if you have a lipsteek. We—Brother Damon does not allow us to use ze make-up. Beside, Lizette, she does not need any lip rouge; her lips, zey are red enough, M'sieur!" She sighed. "Please, what is it you want? I am beezy."

"Where is this place where you are, Lizette?" He tried to be casual.

"Why, Week Harbor, of a certainty."

"Sure, sure. But what part of Long Island?"

"On ze ocean," she said. "Ze South Shore. . . . What you call eet. You weel come out here? You weesh to be saved by Brother Damon? You weesh to be one of ze chosen?"

"Sis," he told her, "I *am* one of the chosen. And I sure would like to be saved —by anyone. Hold ze temple, honey!"

He hung up, then, and stood there for a moment, staring down at the phone, praying that his head would stay in one piece. Then he went into the medicine cabinet and helped himself to a couple of aspirins. He swallowed them with a wicked jolt from the bottle of good bourbon still sitting on the cocktail table.

Harlow picked up the remainder of the fifth and stuck it into his pocket, and left the apartment.

CHAPTER FOUR

Batty Babes

THE cabby who Ben Harlow had bribed at Times Square finally reached the sign for which they had been looking. It read: *Disciples of Damon.* They turned right onto a dirt top road. At the end of the dirt road, they came to a huge private estate, set back from the road and surrounded by a high wall, topped with barbed wire. They drove up before a gate. Harlow got out of the cab. A strong wind whipped at his hair, and whistled through the tall trees that reared over the wall of the estate. Not far off, he could hear the booming of surf. The moon popped out for a moment, from behind scudding clouds and in its wan light, far back of the big gate toward which he was now walking, he saw top of what looked to be a huge, old-fashioned mansion house.

The gate to the estate was of heavy wood and it hurt Harlow's fist to pound on it. No one answered his summons.

Harlow banged on the gate some more but nothing happened. Finally, he gave it up. Walking back to the cab, he saw what looked like the beginning of a footpath, leading into thick clouds beyond. He said to the cabby:

"I'm going to see where that path leads. There'll be another five in it for you—if you wait."

The cabby grunted. "Okay. I'll have a snooze." He snapped off the headlights and settled in his seat.

Harlow moved over onto the grass at the side of the road and ran silently along it toward the path leading into the woods. The moon came out and helped him follow the contours of the path and in a few moments, he was going down a steep embankment and onto a short stretch of beach. Here, the roar of the surf was like the rumbling of continual thunder.

The wind had increased now and was screaming about his ears and whipping flying sand into his face. He looked down the beach a hundred feet or so to where the embankment suddenly became a cliff. Dimly, just back from the top of that cliff, Harlow saw the top outline of the big mansion that was apparently the temple of the Disciples of Damon.

He walked down that way and stood at the foot of the cliff, looking up. There was little beach here and the waves rolled in, right up to where he stood. A few yards farther on, the cliff curved inward and great rollers broke savagely over jagged rocks at the foot of it.

The cliff above Harlow wasn't too high but it was very steep and it would give a man a bad fifteen minutes, climbing it. Especially in this wind. Especially by a man who had been drunk and sobered several times and half-brained with a shovel.

He started the long climb upward. There were plenty of hand and foot holds but some of them were sharp and before he was half way up, Harlow's hands were cut and bleeding. Several times, the wind whipped at him and almost blew him off the cliff. Spray from the breaking waves below doused him. He was trembling and exhausted when he finally scaled the top and stood there, gulping in air.

The moon was quite bright now and Harlow found himself on a plateau. He found himself also confronted by the figure of a young woman, standing a few feet away from him in the moonlight. She was short and dark and the wind whipped at her long, jet black hair and the bangs over her forehead. It plastered the short robe, corded tightly about the waist, close to her sturdy young body.

In the brief moment that they both stared at each other, in speechless shock, Harlow saw that the robe, which ended well above the knees, was embroidered across the front with a partially coiled rattlesnake. The girl's feet were encased in little sandles, bound on with silken ribbons, high above the ankle.

Suddenly, she screamed, a terrible sound that was instantly picked up by the fierce, whipping wind and carried out to sea. Then she thrust something toward him.

At first, Harlow couldn't believe his eyes. He thought for a moment that his many bouts with the bottle had at last finally caught up with him. Because the squirming, writhing thing in the dark girl's hand was a diamond-backed rattlesnake. It darted its head viciously at Harlow. Harlow teetered on the edge of the cliff, almost lost his balance. He yelled at the girl:

"Throw that damned thing away!"

But she ignored him for a moment, continued to hold the snake out before her, in what seemed now to be a protective gesture. He watched it coiling its slippery length affectionately about the girl's forearm. And then she pulled the huge serpent toward her, cuddled it in her arms. She burst out with wild, ringing laughter.

"You look so—so funny! For ze moment, you scared me, but now I see it is you, M'sieur, who ees ze frightened one!"

Harlow recovered a little. He said, hesitantly: "I'd recognize that accent anywhere. You are Lizette, the gal I spoke to on the phone?"

"Oui!" she said and peered at him intently through the moonlight. "Oh, eet is you, ze funny man on ze telephone!" She smiled and her whole, pretty little dark face lighted up. Then she looked down at the rattler she held and stroked it fondly.

"My Henri!" she cooed. "My patron zerpent! The funny man, he is afraid of my nice Henri, non?"

Harlow stared at her, horrified. "Doesn't that damned thing bite you?"

SHE frowned at him. "Oh, non, non, M'sieur! I zee you do not know about thees beautiful zerpents. Brother Damon weel instruct you—when he returns. Then you weel not be afraid of zem, either. And then they weel not bite you. Once you lose your fear of ze zerpents, M'sieur, they will perform miracles for you."

And then Harlow got it. This Disciples of Damon outfit was some fanatical faith-healing cult who used live snakes as their symbol of worship. Harlow kept his distance.

"Look, Lizette," he said. "I'm looking for a friend. I have reason to believe he came here, tonight. He may even be a member of your—your group."

"What ees he look like?"

Swiftly, Harlow described the phony plumber.

Instantly, Lizette said: "Oui! You are describing ze gentleman called Tark. He ees a good friend of our Damon. M'sieur Tark came here tonight weeth ze two beautiful mademoiselles."

"Two girls?" Harlow asked. "What are they like?"

Lizette gave a rough description of Roxy Breen and redheaded Fay Conover.

Harlow felt excitement begin to pound in his head as he asked: "Where can I find this Tark?"

"He ees not a member of our group," Lizette explained. "So he cannot live in ze temple, itself. When he is here, M'sieur Tark lives in the chauffeur's quarters, up over the garage, in the rear of the temple."

Harlow knew of this Tark. The State Department and the FBI were looking for him. Harlow asked Lizette:

"Where is Damon now?"

Lizette said: "Damon and hees disciples have gone on a voyage. Only Lizette here now."

Harlow lit out for the garage on the run, leaving Lizette and her pet serpent there at the cliff edge. This thing was beginning to make sense, now.

There were two large, powerful sedans parked in the garage. Harlow headed toward a wooden stairway that led to the second floor. He went up it, three steps at a time, his heart hammering with excitement and dread.

At the top of the steps, he found a short hall, with doors opening off of it from each side. The first one he came to was open and he stepped inside. It was a very simply furnished bedroom, containing a maple double bed and dresser, and two straight-backed chairs. There was no one in there and Harlow started to leave the room again, when he heard a sound from two closets, side by side, at the far wall of the room. Both the closet doors were closed. The sound had been only faint and it had stopped, but Harlow was certain someone was hiding in one of those closets.

Cautiously, he advanced across the room toward the closet doors. His hand reached out for the knob of the nearest one and a voice from behind Harlow, said:

"Leave that door alone, lover."

He spun around. Standing just inside the room was Roxy Breen. She held a snub-nosed automatic in her hand, pointing at him. She was pale as death. There was a twisted grin on her face and her green eyes held a bright glitter.

The hand that didn't hold the gun was clenched at her side in a fist. Suddenly she pushed it out toward him, opened her fist and showed him the little tube of lipstick lying on her palm. "I got it back, Ben," she said. "They thought they could get it away from me." She giggled and licked at her full lips. "You know what I'm going to do now, lover?"

He shook his head, looking at the gun. He couldn't find his voice to answer.

She said soothingly, gently, "I'm going to kill someone, lover boy. *Me*—Roxy—*I'm* going to kill. This time the souvenir won't be second-hand. I'll have the gun I shot a man to death with! Think of that, lover boy Ben. *Think what that will do for me!*"

He started to put up his hand. He realized that he had helped to nourish this terrible fetish of Roxy's and now it was turning on him, like a monster grown out of hand. Roxy was going to kill *him!*

"Roxy! Don't! *You've gone insane!* You—"

HE BROKE off as the sound of the automatic cracked sharply in the room, echoing back and forth against the walls. Three times in rapid succession, smoke and flame jetted from the stubby muzzle.

At each shot, Harlow jerked and could almost feel the stab of searing pain at his middle. And then, amazingly, he saw that Roxy wasn't pointing the gun quite at him. The angle was off. He realized that she had finished shooting and he was still standing there. She hadn't been shooting at him at all. He watched her in utter fascination. The expression on her face was a terrible thing to see. Then she wheeled and left the room.

Suddenly, to Harlow's ears came the most inhuman scream he had ever heard. It rose to an ear-splitting shriek, then chopped off as if it had been severed by a cleaver. Ice-cold sweat gushed from every pore of Harlow's quivering body.

He drove himself to cross the floor to the door. On the landing outside the door, at the head of the steep flight of wooden steps, he saw Lizette trying to soothe a very ruffled snake.

Lizette tossed her head toward the concrete garage floor at the foot of the stairs. "Zat woman scared my poor Henri. . . ."

Harlow pictured Roxy seeing the diamond-back striking toward her—and her mind, hanging on a shred, had shattered as she lunged into space. He moved woodenly toward the top of the steps and looked down.

Roxy's twisted, broken body could not have housed life. He did not go down to examine her. A strange, free feeling inside him told him that Roxy Breen was dead.

Slowly, Harlow turned back into the room and closed the door. He looked at the door of the closet to his left. There were three bullet holes through it. He saw that the key was still in the outside of the lock and reached out and turned it. Gently he opened the door and Tark, the phony plumber, a foreign automatic clutched against him, all doubled over, tumbled out. Tark's eyes were rolled back in his head. Blood drooled slowly from one corner of his thick mouth. Roxy had done her work well.

And then Harlow jumped, nervously, as there came the sound of a muffled kick, from the other closet. He waited until his nerves quieted and reached out and unlocked that door. He saw a girl, hunched down in there, bound hand and foot, gagged. She was wearing a dark green business suit and her hair was a beautiful sunset red.

"Fay!" He stooped to unfasten her bonds.

When he got the gag off, she said: "Ah, the Marines have landed!"

Harlow said: "What—where—when —and why? . . . Tell it slow and tell it easy."

"After you left Stella Martin's apartment," she said, "I began to work on the knot of that tie you used to bind my hands. In a few minutes, I was free. I went next door. That slinky dame, Roxy, was just conking you with a broken shovel."

Harlow had a dazed grin on his tired face. "Easy!" he said. "Let's get back to the beginning. Who are you, Fay? And that blonde, Stella Martin? Give it to me, slower and easier. My mental processes aren't so good right at this point."

So she told him. She was on a special investigation job for the Petterson, a Newspaper Syndicate, working right inside Tark's headquarters. She had found a weak link in his organization—Stella Martin, from whom she'd been buying information. Fay had finally sold Stella the idea of getting her a list of the names of big American business men who were

sympathetic to a foreign power. These names were listed on a micro film that Stella Martin had smuggled out, hidden in her lipstick.

"I was supposed to get them from her, at her apartment tonight and make the payoff," Fay said. "But Tark beat me to Stella tonight. He shot her before he found out where the film was hidden. He came back later, took Stella's body and put the apartment in order. . . . Now suppose you tell me how you fit into all this, Ben Harlow."

That took some doing, but Harlow finally managed to tell most of the truth. When he finished, he said: "And after you saw Roxy giving me the bang on the skull, what happened?"

Fay said gently: "I tried to get the lipstick from her. But she was like a kid with a stick of candy. Finally, I had to tell her what was in it, what it was all about. Right after that, Tark came to, pulled his gun on us. He and some of his workers brought us out here. Somehow, that Roxy—she was good—tricked Tark into that closet, and slammed the door on him. Then she ran to some other room to get a gun."

"Roxy," Harlow said softly, "is dead." He let out a long, slow breath. "We'll get the lipstick from her."

Harlow remembered the badly punished fifth of bourbon in his coat pocket. He took out the bottle and said to Fay: "Guess we both could use a little snort or so."

She pointed to several glasses over on the dresser. Harlow was moving over toward them when something hit him on the back of his head. The floor came up to meet him. He lay there in a half-world too tired, battered and comfortable to move.

Then he heard Fay's voice close to his ear:

"Well, Mister Rumdum Newshound,

I'll get in my story first. . . . See you around—sometime."

Harlow didn't answer. He just lay there. Presently he heard the roar of one of those powerful sedans down in the garage. He pushed himself to a sitting position, blinked and saw that the bourbon bottle was still intact on the chair where he had left it. He put down a gigantic jolt. Then he saw Lizette come into the room with a petulant Henri wrapped around her arm.

When Lizette saw Harlow sitting on the floor, she tossed Henri onto the bed. Henri lashed around a few times, coiled himself and decided to relax. Lizette kneeled beside Harlow and massaged his head with a gliding, serpentine, hypnotic rhythm.

Harlow grabbed the cool, soft hand and held it in both of his. He asked her:

"Is there a telephone in the temple?"

"*Oui, M'sieur.*"

Harlow grinned lopsidedly. It would be an hour before Fay Conover reached a telephone. His story would be practically on the streets by then. He took another pull at the bourbon.

Lizette leaned close to him and asked: "What ees in zat bottle?" Her imported perfume was a swirling mist around his badly battered head. Harlow managed to say:

"We'll go into zat—later. First, the telephone."

Lizette got to her feet, smoothed the scanty robe over her lithe thighs and smiled down at Harlow.

Harlow climbed to his feet, jerked a thumb at the relaxing Henri on the bed. "What about him?"

Lizette pouted. "Henri has become zee bore. . . . Lizette, she need understanding." She beckoned a finger at him. "Come wiz me."

Harlow tucked the bottle into his pocket, breathed: "Me—and batty babes."

THE END

A Century of the Killer Curse

THE scream ripped through the night like a dagger through black fabric. Josiah Hudson stirred in his sleep, opened his ancient, watery eyes and sat up in the wide bed. A gibbous moon cast her beams through the half-raised window and haloed his hair with silver. Outside the wind moaned faintly and the surf thudded dully against the rocky coast a half-mile away.

The echoes of the scream evanesced in the corridors of the old house. It was followed by a muffled sound of racked sobbing. Josiah Hudson threw back his blankets, shivered, and thrust his thin legs out of the bed. His stiff toes groped on the cold floor for his slippers. He stood up, draped a flannel robe over his bent shoulders, reached for his stick and went out into the hall.

There was no light in the corridor. But Josiah Hudson had lived in this house for sixty-five years and he walked through the darkness with the sureness of a blind man. After eight paces, his hand stretched out and closed without fumbling on the doorknob of the room which his niece, Thelma, shared with her husband, Nick Worthington.

Josiah Hudson entered the vast, old-fashioned bed chamber. The slim body of his niece lay in the huge bed, covered by a single sheet. Her face was buried in the pillow and her fair hair glowed in the illumination of the yellow shaded lamp. Her body moved convulsively. Broken sobs stuttered into Josiah's ears.

On the edge of the bed sat Nick Worthington. His handsome, youthful face was taut with anxiety. His clear eyes were troubled. He looked up as Josiah advanced and silently mouthed a sentence:

"I've phoned for Doc Anders."

Josiah nodded. He came closer to the bed, stared with anxious eyes at Thelma. He said, "What's the matter?"

Nick Worthington made a gesture which adjured Josiah to silence. He said aloud, "Nothing. A slight touch of hysteria. Nothing to worry about."

His wife swung her head around on the pillow. She stared at her uncle. Her face was completely drained of color. Her eyes were wide and flooded with horror.

"Hysteria!" she cried and her voice broke. "Uncle Jo, I've murdered Chippendale."

She buried her face in the pillow once more and sobbed like a tortured child. It was then that Josiah Hudson saw the cat.

Chippendale was not a valuable cat and as feline chronology is considered, she was almost as old as Josiah. She lay on the floor at the side of the bed. She lay in a stiff, distorted position and she lay very still.

By D. L. Champion

Josiah bent down and peered closer. The cat's eyes bulged glassily from her head and her tongue, colored like a bruise, thrust itself grotesquely from her mouth. The fur about her neck was ruffled and awry. Obviously, the animal had been strangled.

Josiah Hudson straightened up. A chill wind swept in from the sea, crossed the window-sill and breathed coldly on the old man's bare legs. A shiver ran through his frame. He became suddenly aware of a sickening emptiness at the pit of his stomach.

He said, "Good Lord, Nick, Thelma didn't do that!"

"Of course not, Uncle Jo. That's what I keep telling her."

The trembling girl turned her head and looked up at them. "There was fur under my nails," she said in a dull monotone. "Chippendale's fur."

"Rot," said Nick and his voice was utterly without conviction. "It's your own hair. You picked it up when you brushed your hair before going to bed."

"And blood," she went on as if he had not spoken. "Look. There's blood on my hand."

She held out her delicate fingers. Josiah saw a tiny red stain at the base of her thumb.

"Nail polish," said Nick. "You spotted yourself when you put it on."

Josiah drew a deep breath. The crimson stain was three shades brighter than the polish on Thelma's nails.

Headlights stabbed the night beyond the window pane. Brakes grated and a car pulled up on the gravel driveway.

"It's Doc Anders," said Nick. "Wait here. I'll let him in."

JOSIAH nodded. As Nick left the room, he seated himself on the edge of the bed. He took his niece's hand in his and stroked it gently. His eyes deliberately avoided the dead cat as his mind deliber-ately avoided all thought, all conjecture.

There was black and evil sap in the Hudson family tree. The insane strain had lain dormant for more than a hundred years until it had evinced itself horribly in Micah, Josiah's great uncle, when Josiah was a lad of sixteen.

A short, gray-haired man came into the room. He said, "Hello, Josiah. Nick's in the library. You'd better join him there. I'll be along later."

Josiah Hudson said, "Very well, Doctor," and left the room. The hall outside was cold and drafty but there was a greater searing chill in the heart of Josiah Hudson.

The library was a huge, rectangular room, three sides of which were lined with books that stretched to the ceiling. Nick Worthington sat in an armchair, staring out the window into the night. He sighed and turned his head as Josiah entered.

"The cook and Jane Harkins are awake," he said. "I've ordered some cof-fee."

Josiah nodded dumbly. His gaze moved to the sideboard where three cut-glass decanters glittered. It was not coffee he needed. Brandy alone would rout the awful coldness within him. He crossed the room and filled a glass.

The liqueur was warm and good on his tongue. Josiah Hudson was a connoisseur of brandy and now he was grateful for the stimulus it imparted to his chilled blood. He put down the glass and seated himself beside Nick Worthington.

"For heaven's sake," he said, "what happened?"

Nick's strained face turned to his. "It was terrible," he said miserably. "I awoke to find her on her knees at the side of the bed. Her hands encircled the cat's throat. She was muttering some awful gibberish. And the expression on her face—on her sweet face, Uncle Jo—it was unbelievable. She looked like some murderous harpy."

"There was fur under my nails—" she said— "and blood. . . ."

Long ago virile Micah Hudson rotted in madhouse chains. And now that same kill-curse was crawling in the mind of a lovely heiress.

His voice broke and he buried his face in his hands.

Josiah Hudson's eyes were bleak and empty. He murmured, "I've been afraid for fifty years. Ever since——"

Nick glanced at him. "You mean Micah? Thelma told me something about him. You mean that maybe——"

The massive door opened and Dr. Anders came into the room. He put his black bag heavily on the floor and came toward them.

Josiah said, "What do you think, Doctor?"

Anders shrugged his shoulders. "I am an old man and only a general practitioner. I don't know much about these things. It is best to get an expert opinion."

Josiah said, "Do you think it is hereditary? Over a hundred years ago, there was Jabez. And in my lifetime there was Micah."

"Perhaps. Eugenics is still something of a mystery."

"What was wrong with Micah?" said Nick harshly. "He was a——a killer, wasn't he?"

Josiah avoided his eyes and looked at Anders.

The doctor said quietly, "He has a right to know, Josiah."

Josiah Hudson nodded. He cleared his throat and spoke slowly and reluctantly. "Micah Hudson was my great uncle. He was a huge man, well over six feet. He was kind and gentle, and as a child I loved him. When I was sixteen, they took Micah away. They took him away in chains and a straight-jacket. They said he was a homicidal maniac."

Nick stared at him, wide-eyed. "You mean he actually committed homicide?"

"He first killed a dog. It was my dog and I loved it. Micah murdered it with his bare hands. I thought at the time that nothing worse could ever happen. But it did. His second victim was our house-maid. After that, they took him away, my Uncle Micah. I know nothing of the condition of asylums today but then they were vermin-infested death traps. They took him away and chained him to a post in a common room peopled with a hundred shrieking maniacs.

"They neither washed him nor fed him decently. I saw him once before he died —a dirt encrusted, hairy old man with the horror of Hell, itself, in his rheumy, sunken eyes."

Nick Worthington's face was an ashen mask. He said hoarsely, "Doctor, you don't think that Thelma——"

"Get an expert," said Doctor Anders. "Get the best opinion there is."

"I know a man," said Nick suddenly. "He's considered very good. He——"

"Don't bother with a man who's very good," said Anders. "Money is secondary with you people. Get the best there is. Get Weldon."

There was a moment's silence. "Can we get him?" asked Josiah. "I've heard of him. He's the most famous psychiatrist in the country. He's a busy man. Can we get him at once?"

Anders opened his mouth to speak but before he uttered a word, Nick said, "I'll get him. One of the clients of our advertising agency plays golf with him. I'll get Weldon."

"Good," said Anders. "You can accept Weldon's opinion as Gospel."

Josiah moved uneasily in his chair. "Anders," he said, "do you really believe that she is——" it took an effort for him to pronounce the final word—"mad?"

"If she is not," said Anders, "brooding upon this thing as she has done will make her so."

Josiah Hudson drew a deep breath. There flashed across his mind a vivid picture of a half-naked, chained old man with black and burning eyes. He said fervently, "I would rather see her dead than like Micah."

There was a taut silence in the room, then the thin, frightened voice of Jane Harkins, the maid, said, "Here is the coffee, gentlemen."

JOSIAH HUDSON'S niece and himself were the sole remaining members of a once flourishing family. His delight at her marriage some eight months ago was engendered by the fact that he believed that her children would some day inhabit this ancient, desolate house, bringing back some of its former life and gaiety.

Now all such hope had abandoned him. His head whirred; his aged body trembled. He groped for his stick and returned to his bedroom.

Josiah Hudson passed the following day in dazed misery. Almost every hour he tiptoed to Thelma's room only to find her sleeping restively.

Nick returned from the advertising agency in the late afternoon. He nodded to Josiah, then went at once to his wife's bedroom.

The two men ate their dinners in silence. Over the coffee, Nick spoke. "Well, we'll soon know. I've fixed things up with Weldon's office."

Josiah nodded dully. He was afraid that he knew already.

Nick handed him a slip of paper. "We're to call Weldon tomorrow for an appointment. I've got to do some business in the morning. Will you phone him? The number's there. Have him call as soon as possible. I'll be home early."

Josiah took the slip of paper, folded it and put it in his pocket. He went to bed early but slept little.

Once during the night, he thought he heard a cry. He sat up in bed and listened with all his being. It was not repeated. He lay down again and closed his eyes. Dawn paled the sky and still he had not slept.

He was drinking strong black coffee in the dining room when Nick came down to breakfast. Josiah glanced up and the matutinal greeting froze on his lips. Nick wore no tie and his shirt was open at the throat. Around his neck was a bandage.

Josiah Hudson stared and blinked his eyes. He said in a quavering voice, "Nick! Not you! She didn't—"

Nick Worthington nodded miserably. "I awoke to find her clawing at my throat. But she didn't know what she was doing, Uncle Jo. She was asleep while she was doing it. I'll swear she didn't realize what she was doing."

"Neither did Micah," said Josiah with dull resignation. He got up from the table. "I'm going to phone the doctor now. The sooner he comes, the better."

The maid announced Doctor Noble Weldon shortly after lunch. He was a squat little man with a Van Dyke beard and a brusque manner. He smoked an excellent cigar as he listened to what Josiah told him of Thelma Worthington, Micah Hudson and the monstrous case history of an ancestor who had lived more than a hundred years ago.

He frowned, coughed, asked to see his patient alone. He spent a good half hour in Thelma's bedroom while Josiah sat in the library staring out the window at a gloomy autumnal landscape.

Weldon returned to the library and delivered his opinion without preamble. "It is a rare, though well-documented form of insanity," he said. "A form of schizophrenia, split personality. That in itself is common enough. However, in this instance the savage sadistic urge comes upon her only while she sleeps. She commits these outrages somnambulistically. Awake, her natural and normal instincts are powerful enough to combat the evil which is latent within her. That is not the case when her conscious mind is sleeping."

Josiah said unhappily, "What are we to do, Doctor?"

"I can not answer for what may happen

if she remains here, even under the care of a professional nurse. She must go to a sanatorium. I understand you are well off. I suggest she go to a place I can highly recommend, a private establishment run by an excellent doctor."

Josiah said, "Is there any—any hope that she will recover?"

"There is always hope," said Weldon. "I have spoken to her. She knows she is ill. She is quite willing to go away. It would be well if both you and her husband signed the commitment papers."

"Anything you suggest," said Josiah. "Where is this sanitorium?"

"Twelve miles from town. It is run by Dr. Springer, an excellent man. If anyone can help her, he can. I'll send you the necessary papers in a day or so. Then her husband can take her there. I shall make the arrangements."

"Is there anything we can do for her in the meanwhile?"

Weldon shook his head. "Medicine is of no use in a case such as this."

"There is brandy in the cellar," said Josiah. "Brandy two hundred years old. That wouldn't harm her?"

"By all means, give her the brandy," said Weldon. "Especially if she is faint. Old brandy has a remarkably salutary and revivifying effect."

When Weldon had gone, Josiah quietly opened the door of his niece's bedroom. She apparently was awake but she did not look at him. Her face was white as a gardenia. She stared hopelessly at the ceiling. Josiah watched her for a moment and his heart was wrung.

He closed the door silently, then made his way through the corridors of the old house and descended to the cellar. He came into the library again bearing a cobwebbed bottle. He laid it carefully on the sideboard.

It was four o'clock when Nick Worthington arrived. Josiah greeted him gravely.

"Nick," he said, "it's bad. She—"

Nick said, "I know. I called Weldon at his office. I suppose we've got to do as he says."

"We have no choice, my boy."

Nick nodded dumbly.

"Oh," said Josiah, "you see that bottle on the sideboard? It's brandy. It was bought by my grandfather and it was old when he bought it. The doctor said it might do her some good. At least, it might bring some color to her cheeks."

Nick said, "Thanks," in the tone of a man who is not listening.

JOSIAH HUDSON ate a late breakfast. Nick had left for his office some two hours before. Josiah sipped his coffee without tasting it, found no savor in his boiled egg. Idly he turned the pages of the morning paper propped up against the silver coffee pot.

He was far too preoccupied with his own affairs to pay much attention to those of the world in general. On the third page, however, his eye caught an item which interested him. The County Medical Association had given a dinner the previous evening in honor of Dr. Noble Weldon. Josiah read the report slowly.

He finished the story and had pushed the paper away from him when a thought came to him. He seized the paper again and examined the type carefully. The story stated that Dr. Weldon's office was situated in downtown Grand Street.

Josiah knew that neighborhood. Moreover, he knew quite well that the telephone exchange for that part of town was Evergreen. Yet the number he had called when summoning Weldon had been Royal 6657.

It was unimportant, he thought, but it aroused his curiosity. He went out to the hall and procured a telephone book. He turned to the W's. Dr. Weldon's office number was Evergreen 9080. Directly below it was listed his suburban home, the exchange for which was Humphrey.

Josiah blinked. He picked up the news-paper again. Listed there were the three hospitals with which Weldon was connected. It was quite likely, he considered, that he had reached Weldon at one of these. Slowly he looked up the telephone number of each hospital. None of them was in the Royal exchange.

For a moment he was puzzled. Then he put the whole thing out of his head and poured himself another cup of coffee. But the odd circumstance of those telephone numbers kept recurring to him. His puzzlement grew to a vague, uneasy suspicion.

At twelve o'clock he knew what he must do. He went upstairs to his room and dressed carefully. Then he went out of the house, called a taxicab, and drove to Dr. Weldon's office on Grand Street.

A few minutes later he found himself in an elegantly furnished reception room facing an even more elegant receptionist.

He bowed with old fashioned formality and said, "I want to see Dr. Weldon."

The girl looked up at him. "Have you an appointment?"

"No. But I must see him. At once."

"I'm sorry. I'm afraid—"

"It is a matter," said Josiah Hudson, "of life and death.

There was a searing sincerity in the words. The girl looked at him oddly for a moment, then stood up. "Come this way," she said.

* * *

Josiah Hudson emerged into the chill wind of Grand Street and huddled, momentarily helpless, against the building. What little physical courage he had was almost gone. His mind refused to function. His senses were the confused senses of a drunken man. But desperation impelled him.

He *must* see Nick. Nick would explain things to him. On the other hand, perhaps Nick—but he dared not think of that.

Nick Worthington was not in his office. An efficient stenographer explained that Mr. Worthington had had an appointment and doubtless would go to lunch before he returned. Josiah Hudson left the building.

He knew Nick was in the habit of lunching in the grill room of the Leighton Hotel. He marched to his destination like an ancient scarecrow, his coat flapping in the wind.

He entered the grill and looked around with wild eyes. He did not see Nick Worthington. He approached the head waiter, and asked:

"Has Mr. Worthington been in for lunch?"

The waiter shook his head. "Not yet, sir. Perhaps he is in his suite."

Josiah blinked. "He has a suite here? I thought he lived in the suburbs."

"He does, sir. He keeps the suite to rest in during the afternoon. Mrs. Worthington joins him when she is in town, I believe."

"Mrs. Worthington?"

The head waiter had flitted away to greet a middle-aged couple.

Josiah Hudson left the grill and went into the lobby. In response to his query the clerk said, "Mrs. Worthington? Suite 1200, sir."

Josiah walked to the elevator. His heart was thudding against his chest and his eyes were wide with something close to panic. His gnarled knuckles beat against a door marked 1200.

A blonde opened the door. She was a well-built woman with black eyes which were heavy with mascara. There was a trifle too much makeup on her face, and there was a hard line to her lips.

Josiah said, "Are you Mrs. Worthington?"

"Sure," said the blonde. "What about it, mister?"

"Are—are you Mrs. *Nick* Worthington?"

"That's right. What do you want?"

"Nothing," said Josiah Hudson and fled down the hall.

He was no longer a rational being. He knew that ominous danger hung over his niece's head. He was rather less aware of the sudden threat to himself. He knew he must get home. He must get Thelma out of that house, away from the monstrous evil which was about to envelope her.

He fought his way on a crowded bus, closed his eyes and clung to a strap. An awful knowledge burned into his brain—a knowledge he was terrified to contemplate.

HE ENTERED the old house at a dogtrot. He ran up the stairs and went to Nick's room. He searched the bathroom medicine chest feverishly. Then, in a bottom bureau drawer he found what he had feared he would find.

It was a small square box containing pink capsules. Its label read: *Seconal.*

He put the box in his pocket and ran out into the hall. As he did so, he heard Nick's car coming up the driveway. Panic was suddenly upon him. He raced like a scared child into his own room, locked the door behind him.

He remained there for twenty minutes trying desperately to summon the last reserves of his courage. He knew he was very close to death and he knew he was in all likelihood a physical coward. But he was not a moral one and more than his own life was at stake.

He stood up. He buttoned his coat about him. He squared his shoulders pitifully and walked down the stairs to the library. The muscles of his stomach were constricted and his heart thudded against his thin chest.

Nick Worthington was standing at the sideboard. He turned his head as Josiah seated himself in a leather arm chair. Josiah stared at him. He wondered vaguely how he had ever thought Nick handsome. Now, those blue eyes which had once seemed gay and laughing were cold and relentless as the Polar Sea. His full red lips were sensual and cruel. Lines of dissipation which Josiah had not observed before were etched deeply in his features.

Josiah said in a voice he fought to keep steady, "Nick, I have something to say to you."

Nick Worthington laughed without mirth. "I have something to say to you, too. You've been snooping in my affairs today. I gather you've been digging in my bureau. You've also seen my girl, haven't you?"

Josiah nodded. "I've seen Doctor Weldon as well."

Nick frowned. "What did you tell him?"

"Nothing. I saw him only long enough to know he is not the man who came here to treat Thelma."

There was a long silence. A flurry of rain pattered against the windows. The ancient grandfather clock ticked imperviously. Josiah Hudson felt a great need to cry out, a tremendous urge to flee from the house. The tight reign of his reason held his emotions in check like a savage bit holding a spirited horse.

"And," said Nick easily, "I assume you have reached certain conclusions?"

"I have," said Josiah. "After I had seen the doctor, it occurred to me that you wanted Thelma committed to an asylum in order to get her money. I knew she trusted you. You had but to ask for it and you could have had her whole fortune."

"So you decided I didn't want her money?"

"No," said Josiah. "I decided you wanted her money and that other girl as well." His calm cracked like a levee in flood time. "How could you do it?" he cried. He took the sleeping pills from his pocket and flung them on the table.

"Night after night you've drugged that girl into uneasy sleep. You killed a cat and scarred your own throat, then told her she had done it. You put blood on her hands and fur under her nails. My God, were you trying to drive her mad?"

"Not necessarily," said Nick. "If she'd gone mad, so much the better. I wanted to send her to Springer's place. That was all."

Josiah Hudson's entire body trembled. "What are you saying!"

"I'll say it all," said Nick Worthington. "It's simple enough. I love that other girl. Not Thelma. But I'm not going to give up Thelma's money. Nor yours either. I knew about Micah and the insane streak in the family. I did what I did to have Thelma committed."

"But if you divorced her on the ground she was insane you'd lose your right to her money."

Nick eyed him coolly. "What gives you the impression that she'd live too long in that madhouse? Micah didn't. Springer will take care of that. I'm paying well."

Josiah shuddered.

Nick went on:

"No one would have questioned anything except, perhaps you. I took care to allay your suspicions. You even would have signed the commitment papers."

"That's why you pretended that man was Weldon?"

"Of course. Anders said Weldon's opinion was gospel. I wanted to avoid any suspicion from you. I reasoned that no one ever checks on a phone number if someone else gives it to him. When you thought you called Weldon, you called Springer at his home. The secretary knew what to do when someone asked for Weldon. An opinion which you and Anders believed came from the great Weldon would keep all suspicion from me when I inherited Thelma's money—and yours."

"You—you could do that to Thelma?" Josiah's voice was a dry husk.

"WHY not? The most important thing in the world to me is my own life—to live it as I see fit."

Josiah closed his eyes for a moment. A sudden thought occurred to him.

"How do you dare tell me all this? I'll testify against you."

"You'll testify against no one this side of hell," said Nick Worthington. "Your spying today has compelled me to change my plans, to take more direct action."

Josiah Hudson said nothing. His thin fingers tightened on the arms of his chair. Nick pointed to the cobwebbed brandy bottle on the sideboard. Josiah noticed that its cork had been removed.

"That bottle has been touched by no one but yourself," said Nick. "The glass at its side I took from your room. It doubtless has your fingerprints on it. Holding that bottle with a handkerchief I am going to pour a drink from that bottle into that glass. I am going to give it to Thelma with your compliments."

Josiah gasped, "You've poisoned it!"

"Right. I took some cyanide from the photographic room at the agency. I have dumped it into that brandy. Recall now, you said before two witnesses—Doc Anders and the maid, Jane Harkins—that you'd sooner see Thelma dead than crazy. What more likely than you mercifully poisoned her?" Nick paused for a long time. His hand thrust itself into his coat pocket and withdrew an automatic. Then he added quietly, "And blew your own brains out afterwards."

What Josiah did was sheer physical and nervous reflex. His brain was paralyzed. He uttered a terrible shriek. His clawing fingers reached out and seized a heavy glass ash tray. He hurled the ash tray directly at Nick.

The hurtling object struck Nick in the chest. He staggered back under its impact and his head struck hard against the edge of the marble mantelpiece.

The library door flew open. Jane Harkins ran into the room. She stared at the unconscious form of Nick Worthington. She said, "Mr. Josiah, what's wrong? I heard Mr. Worthington cry out."

Josiah Hudson caught his panting breath. He pulled himself together and said, "He's had a slight accident. I think he's unconscious."

The girl stared about the room. Her eyes fell on the old brandy bottle. She said, "Shall I pour him some brandy before I call the doctor?"

On Josiah Hudson's next words hung a human life. He who had never harmed a living creature, hesitated.

It didn't matter much what happened to him. He had lived his life. But there was still Thelma. He would do what he must do and await the judgment of a merciful God.

"Brandy?" he said in a voice he scarcely recognized as his own. "Of course, give him brandy. I have it on the word of Mr. Worthington's personal physician that brandy has a remarkable salutary and revivifying effect."

THE PERFECT GIFT

A Storiette by John Bender

THE MUSIC of the Montmarte café blasted the flimsy walls, and while Girond watched, Suzanne inspected the green stone necklace in her dressing-room mirror. "It looks so real, my love!"

Girond touched his tiny beard, his eyes hungry upon her. "Your precious Henri does not suspect?"

"That we sell his jewelry?" She drew her filmy robe tighter. "No—he is a stupid pig."

Soon, Henri would arrive. With, Suzanne hoped, the new necklace he had mentioned. It was good, she thought, to be young and lovely, and desired by the handsome Girond—and by such a pig as Henri. A pig whose clever hands could fashion such lovely jewelry!

Already—against the day when she and Girond could leave this filthy music-hall for the Riviera's splendor—she had thousands of francs, obtained by selling Henri's jewelry through Girond, almost as soon as Henri gave it to her. Henri did not demand she wear it often, and Suzanne was clever enough to detract his close inspection away from the simulated pieces.

Henri was due momentarily. With a fervent kiss, Suzanne sent Girond away, and was seated at her dressing table when she heard the knock. The timid knock of Henri.

In her mirror she saw him enter—a paunchy, little fellow with workman's hands. He closed the door and came to stand behind her.

"My dear!" She feigned surprise, though he always acted so, when he had a gift for her. "Something for me, cher?"

She saw him nod, almost to himself. "Something just for you," he whispered strangely. "For you alone—" He broke off.

Suzanne forced a smile. "A surprise?" She dropped her robe, making her white shoulders a temptation for his eyes. "A new necklace?"

She chuckled inwardly thinking him the fool as he reached into his pocket. She closed her eyes, lest he see her eagerness; then she felt, with sudden fear, not the smooth filigreed jewelry, but a scratching, heavy something encircling her neck.

And in the mirror, horrified, she saw this necklace—a neatly-fashioned rope, a hangman's noose—tightening on her throat. . . .

Strangler's Moon

By Curt Hamlin

Garroted women, all strangers to him, were his stepping stones to heights of homicide.

MR. WEMME found the fourth body. There were five in all. The circumstances surrounding each murder were similar. In each instance, a woman was murdered. Never was there an apparent motive. The murdered always used a piece of common cord as his weapon, looping it around the neck of the victim and quickly drawing tight. He always struck on the night of a full moon.

The police quite logically deduced that all of the murders were the work of one man. The police were wrong.

Mr. Wemme found the fourth body because he happened to glance up the narrow alley which ran between High Street and Wilmington Avenue. It was choked with refuse cans, overflowing garbage, and it cast off the sickly sweet smell of decaying food and damp paper. Mr. Wemme invariably crossed its entrance quickly, nose buried in his handkerchief. What made him look up on that particular morning, he never knew.

The woman lay on her right side, with

◆ ◆ ◆

The cord looped in his hands like a live thing....

73

her left arm thrown up so that it covered her face. A length of cord was still wound tight around her neck.

This was an eventful day for Mr. Wemme—for on this same day he met John Denton. He met him partly because he found the fourth body, and partly because Denton looked very much like Mr. Wemme. It was a little after seven in the morning when Mr. Wemme found the body. It was nearly nine that night when Denton rang his front door bell.

Mr. Wemme, a widower, answered the door himself. It was a wild night. The wind shrieked along the eaves and hammered at the windows, setting the panes to a noisy rattling.

A small man with a large mustache stood, hat in hand, on the doorstep. "Mr. Wemme?"

"Yes."

"If I might come in, please." It was a mild, soft voice.

Mr. Wemme stood to one side. He shut the door. "It's warmer in the parlor. I've a fire going." He led the way.

The man with the mustache went directly to the fireplace. He stood before it, arms outstretched, turning his hands this way, and that, to catch the heat. "Nasty night out. Windy."

"Yes."

"Nice place you have here. Can't stand modern stuff." The stranger moved a little from the fire, staring at a display of wax flowers under a dusty glass hood. "My mother had one like that."

"My wife bought it," said Mr. Wemme.

"You're married?" The question was unexpectedly sharp.

Mr. Wemme shook his head. "I was. She's dead, you know."

"Ah."

"Yes."

"I see. I see."

"Well—?" said Mr. Wemme.

The visitor suddenly wiggled out of his overcoat, laid it with his hat on the tufted sofa. "My name's Denton. John C. Denton."

Mr. Wemme murmured that he was Charles R. Wemme.

"Fine." Denton rubbed his hands together briskly. He sat down, drawing a chair close to the fire. "Now we'll talk."

Mr. Wemme also sat down. He was quite puzzled. "Talk?"

"About the body you found." Denton leaner closer, tapped Mr. Wemme impressively on the knee. "That's why I came, you know. About the body."

Mr. Wemme's mouth hung open. "You're from the police?"

Denton chuckled. "My dear Wemme, do I look like a policeman?" He giggled a little. "The fact is—I'm a hobbyist."

"Hobbyist?"

"You know. Stamps. Model planes. Rare books. Pastime. Avocation." He looked up. "You understand, don't you?"

Mr. Wemme shook his head.

Denton's mustache jerked with exasperation. "Here," he said sharply. "It's simple enough. My hobby is murder."

MR. WEMME tried to speak, but his tongue was dry and his lips were stiff and awkward.

Denton was again staring dreamily into the fire. "That's why I came to see you."

"But I don't see—"

"Eh? Found the body, didn't you?" he went on before Mr. Wemme could answer. "I have a theory about the murder. So we'll work together. Catch the murderer, I mean. Quite a feather."

The feeling of fantasy grew. Mr. Wemme felt helpless, trapped. "But the police—"

"The police," said Denton coldly, "are fools." His hand darted inside his coat, burrowed about, came up clutching a ragtag assortment of newspaper clippings. "Now then. The facts." He balanced a pince-niz on the tip of his nose and read rapidly. "Salient points. Four murders.

Always women. No motive. Night of the full moon. Uses cord." He reached into another pocket. "Like this."

Mr. Wemme took it. It was a length of stout butcher's cord, knotted at each end to keep it from ravelling. He looked numbly down at the cord. "I suppose the murderer is insane. He would be, wouldn't he?"

"You're wrong!"

Denton was so abrupt and vehement that Mr. Wemme started quite violently.

"Never trust the obvious, Wemme. Besides, it's perfectly clear that the murderer is a man of superior intelligence."

"Really?" A dazed expression was spreading over Mr. Wemme's small, pink features. "I'm afraid I don't follow you."

"Think, man." Denton jumped from his chair, paced excitedly back and forth in front of the fireplace. "First, the lack of motive. Of course he has a motive. But he's kept it hidden." His voice dropped dramatically. "Clever, Wemme. Very clever. This man plans. When he goes out to murder—" Denton snatched up the cord—"he takes this. You know how he uses it?"

"Well, I—"

"Like this." Denton made a loop. He made it expertly, with a jerk of his wrists. He swooped suddenly forward. The loop dropped over Mr. Wemme's head, tightened with a snap at his throat. For one horrible moment he was gasping for breath. Then the pressure was gone, and Denton had dropped back exhaustedly in his chair.

"You see?"

"Terrible." Mr. Wemme swabbed his forehead.

"Exactly."

"But the business about a full moon? And the motive. If he's sane, he must have a motive."

"That," said Denton softly, "is the cleverest part of all. The police are looking for a man who kills without motive."

He turned his round, glowing eyes on Mr. Wemme. "Suppose that for *one* of these murders, there is a motive. Who would suspect, Wemme? Who would suspect? Think of it! To commit murder and walk away free."

He left, then. His going was as abrupt and unexpected as his coming. He stood up, put on his coat, picked up his hat. Mr. Wemme accompanied him into the hall. At the door, Denton paused and shook hands. "Think about it," he urged. "Keep it in mind. I'll be back."

He disappeared into the night.

Mr. Wemme returned to the parlor. The fire had died down. The room was cold, with shadows in the corners. He decided to go up to bed, switched off the light and climbed the narrow, dark stairway to the second floor. In his dresser mirror he saw that Denton's cord noose still hung about his neck. He snatched it off and flung it from him. The thing dropped in twisted layers, like some pale, revolting reptile coiled to spring. Mr. Wemme kicked at it gingerly, pushing it out of sight under the bed.

His dreams that night were hideous.

DURING the next four weeks Mr. Wemme was extraordinarily nervous. Dreams disturbed him. His brain bubbled with every manner of strange fantasy. He plotted dark plots, and thought weird, unholy thoughts.

Most of the time, of course, he was quite normal, and the fantastic vagaries of his mind seemed remote and unreal. Nevertheless, he felt a constant and mounting excitement that sucked like an undertow, pulling him into the depths that were both forbidden and fascinating.

For one reason or another, he expected Denton to come back on the night of the full moon. He didn't take off his shoes that evening, and he kept his coat on and his vest properly buttoned. He was in a restless mood. He glanced at his watch,

He piled wood on the fire. He drew back the window drapes to look out at the weather. It was fine and clear. The moon was huge—a great, round, yellow globe.

Denton came at nine.

He marched right in without ringing the bell, dropping his hat and coat on the sofa. He greeted Mr. Wemme with an airy wave of his hand. "Can't stay long. Meeting my wife. Lovely night, isn't it? Very." He plumped down into his chair, giggling. "For a murder. Lovely night for a murder."

Mr. Wemme watched anxiously. "Have you discovered anything?"

"Nothing. Not a thing. Not even one thing." Denton held up a finger. "Have to get him next time."

"Next time?"

"Keep trying, you know. That's the trick." The strange eyes turned on Mr. Wemme. "Been thinking?"

"Some. Quite a little." Mr. Wemme smiled shyly. "To tell you the truth, I could hardly get it out of my head. What you said about committing murder, I mean."

"Yes."

"I—it must have made quite an impression."

"Yes."

Mr. Wemme fidgeted nervously under the steady, unwinking gaze of the luminous eyes. "All nonsense, of course."

"Nonsense?" Denton's voice was quite sharp. "Not at all, Wemme. Not at all. On the contrary. Serious. Quite."

"But it isn't right," Mr. Wemme protested weakly. "Murder shouldn't be—"

"Fascinating? But it is. Isn't it? Admit it. Admit it, Wemme. Dammit, I don't mind. Strikes me the same way. Well?"

"Well—"

"Of course. Quite right." Denton's hand shot suddenly into a pocket. He thrust a package under Mr. Wemme's nose. "Cigarette?"

Mr. Wemme held up his pipe. "I usually—"

"Try one. Special blend. Made for me." He pressed a paper cylinder into Mr. Wemme's hand, produced a match, struck it noisily with his thumbnail. "Light up."

Mr. Wemme did. He thought the cigarette had an odd flavor. It made him cough.

"Draw it in," said Denton. "Draw it in. Turkish tobacco. Good for the lungs."

Mr. Wemme drew in. The smoke was heavy. It hung in a cloud around his head. He felt faintly dizzy.

Denton's voice seemed to be moving further and further away. "Keep drawing. Good, eh?"

Mr. Wemme said, "Good." He had an extraordinary sensation of floating, as though he was rising above the Morris chair on a comfortable air cushion.

DENTON seemed to be calling from infinite distance. "Draw it in. Draw it in." His voice was so faint that Mr. Wemme turned his head to make sure his visitor was not leaving. A pair of incredibly large, blindingly bright eyes were peering at him from a point just beyond his own nose. A voice, something like Denton's voice, said, "There'll be a murder tonight. Must meet my wife. She's waiting. Not safe for her."

"Headache," Mr. Wemme said simply.

"Of course. Take a walk with me. Clear your head." Denton's fingers closed firmly over his arm. "Coat. Chilly out. Where is it?"

"Hall."

The coat seemed heavy. Leaden. They went outside. To Mr. Wemme, the porch steps were ten feet high. He floated down them softly. Denton kept urging him on. "Walk fast. That'll clear your head."

They hurried along the sidewalk by tremendous bounds and leaps, sailing up without effort and coasting gently down.

At the alley between High Street and Wilmington Avenue, Denton stopped. "It happened here—last month."

Mr. Wemme looked up the dark ravine of the alley. It stretched endlessly. "Here."

"With one of these."

Denton dangled a piece of butcher's cord. Mr. Wemme took it from him. It was enormously long, but his arms were somehow longer. "Yes."

"And he got away."

Mr. Wemme said, ". . .he got away."

"Interesting, eh?"

"Yes."

"We'd better hurry. My wife will be waiting. Can't keep her waiting. Here. Give me your arm."

They went on. The cord still dangling from Mr. Wemme's fingers. Denton's voice murmured at his ear. "A clever man could get away with it. They'd blame the *other one*, of course. This is his night, you know."

They hurdled a curb. Mr. Wemme said, "Yes."

"Think of it. Think of it. Think of it—" The murmur undulated off into the distance, and was gone.

Mr. Wemme stepped over a very large match on the sidewalk.

Denton said, "An uncontrollable impulse. To kill, that is. It must be a woman, though. You understand, don't you? Not a young woman. Middle-aged. Ugly." Denton stopped suddenly, dragging Mr. Wemme to a halt beside him. "How's the headache?"

"Headache?" He thought for a moment. "I feel fine."

"Nothing like a walk. Clears your head. Got to leave you here. Better walk a little further. Look! Up there on the next corner. A woman, isn't it?" It was a woman. She stood under a street lamp, waiting. Denton's tone took on a feverish excitement. "Must be an old woman, Wemme.

Not young. Get away with it, of course. Fascinating, isn't it? Remember the cord."

"Why?"

"Go it, Wemme." Denton was easing away. "Go it. Don't forget."

Mr. Wemme looked up along the long block to where the woman stood. He turned his head, looked at Denton's receding figure. He nodded. The cord looped in his hands like a live thing. He began to run silently. After a moment he said, almost thoughtfully, "Why?"

No one answered. Denton was quite beyond hearing.

* * *

They caught Wemme. He was dragging the body down High Street, toward the alley, when he was arrested. He cried bitterly, reproaching himself for having made a terrible mistake. He was too shaken to answer questions. They put him in a cell and he lay down on the straw mattress and fell immediately into the heavy sleep of innocent exhaustion. His pink face was relaxed and unlined. The Chief Inspector looked in at him through the bars. "Doped to the ears."

"What is it?" asked the district attorney.

"Marijuana."

"Wonder where he got it?"

"We'll ask him that when he wakes up. It isn't important, though. The important thing is that we finally caught him."

The district attorney lit a cigar, puffed it with comfortable pleasure. "Just the same, it took you a long time. He got five of them. Let's see. There was Combs, Howard, Tate, Prentiss. . ."

"And Denton."

"Yes. Funny thing, the way the last one he picked was a man. And there was this Denton's wife just around the block from where it happened, waiting on the corner. Isn't that the damndest coincidence?"

The chief inspector said it was.

... Crypt of the Jealous Queen

His vain wife flew out of his life on butterfly wings ... strewing her vengeance with a cobra's venom.

DAVE drove up and jumped out of his car. I waited at the ivy covered gate, and we went up the brick walk together.

"I don't get this, Solly," said Dave as we climbed the gray stone steps to the front porch. "I don't get this deal at all."

I pushed the doorbell, kept my voice low.

"There might be something to it. We'll know in a minute."

The man who opened the door was small, lean, about fifty-five, with a jungle of short brown hair. The hairline was low, and the forehead slightly recessive. Steel spectacles framed electric-green eyes.

"Dr. Kreutch?" I asked.

He stared at us a moment, then a shadow of a smile passed across his face and his head inclined courteously.

"I am Dr. Kreutch." The voice was deep, quiet, and the articulation was precise. "Come in, gentlemen. I've been expecting you. Come in."

Dave glanced at me quickly. There had been no advance notice of our call. But Dr. Kreutch had already turned and was walking slowly down the long, gloomy hallway. There was nothing to say, nothing to do but follow him. I heard Dave close the front door as he trailed along.

Dr. Kreutch walked ahead of me as if he were tired, his head and round shoulders bent forward, his long arms relaxed, hanging loose, the hands turned inward and up after the manner of an anthropoid ape. I remembered the hair line, too, and the forehead—but then I thought of the electric-green eyes.

He led us silently through the long hall, and into a spacious drawing room. It was an old room, carpeted in lush olive green, and paneled in a dark hardwood, probably teak.

He walked without pause, and we followed him over the entire length of the drawing room until he came to a heavy, vaulted door. Here he stopped, stood pensively stroking his chin.

"Dr. Kreutch," I said, "perhaps we should introduce—"

He interrupted me with a gesture. Again I saw that peculiar shadow of a smile at his lips.

"Please," he said. "If you will permit me. First, there is something to attend to." He turned, wrenched open the heavy door. "Step in quickly, please." He disappeared into the darkness.

Dave and I pushed after him, stopped short. The door closed ponderously behind us.

The room was dark, very dark. The atmosphere was thick with the musty, torpid odor of decaying leaves or strange jungle blossoms.

She was reaching for the second one, when I took her throat in my hands.

Then a lamp clicked on. We saw him bending over a small desk in the center of a huge, crypt-like room.

We stood motionless, staring.

That room! Walled with the rarest flowers and vines—hundreds of them. Shelf upon shelf of bowls, urns, and elaborate vases, and in front of the shelves, a narrow, continual table burdened with glass cases and aquariums, some empty, others magnifying delicate submerged plants through whose intertwines swam scores of brilliantly colored fish.

The room's one window was completely blinded by a black shade.

Dr. Kreutch had crossed to stand perfectly still before two glass cases, both of which appeared empty. He sighed.

79

"My only commoners—these two."

Dave's breath came harshly into my ear. "He's mad. He's utterly mad."

"The cobra requires more than five thousand human lives each year, to justify his existence."

We saw it then, in the near case, rising gracefully from the dirt—the swaying hood of the King Cobra.

"And this little one. . . . Who knows how many lives the Krait requires?"

We stepped forward impulsively, peered into the second case. It was a small, worm-like snake, thick as a cigar, and no longer than fourteen inches. An orange stripe ran the length of him down his back.

"The Krait, gentlemen. After his kiss, a man may survive from forty seconds to as long as two and a half minutes.

I SHUDDERED. For an instant I saw the green eyes of Dr. Kreutch fixed on the Krait with fierce, hypnotic pleasure. Then, gradually, his face softened, and he sighed again.

"Ah well. Business waits upon the eccentricities of the host. Very well. I shan't be long. Come, gentlemen. This is my—" he smiled apologetically— "greatest achievement."

We followed him to the desk where he bent down and opened the bottom drawer. When he straightened, I saw that he was holding carefully an ordinary two-quart jar. He lifted it to his eyes, and then he moved off toward the window, carrying it gently—as gently as though it contained something infinitely precious.

At the window, he set down the jar. He rolled up the blind the pushed open the window in one gesture. Then he lifted the jar, his hands shaking, so that the sunlight slanted sharply, flashed chromatically through the glass.

"Gentlemen," he said very softly. "Gentlemen, the Queen."

As if responding to the introduction, there arose fluttering from the bottom of the jar, the most beautiful butterfly in the world.

The upper wings measured probably six inches from tip to tip. Begining close to the body, they were the deepest sapphire blue, fading imperceptibly lighter through all the blues until at the wing edges the color had paled to silver. The wing perimeters were traced with a thin line of arterial red. And the borderline carried completely around the lower wings as well, which were rich gold in color, and were dotted with four pairs of blue pinhead dots.

The body of the insect was silver, patterned with duplicate arabesques of cerise twining upward from the end of the abdomen, and terminating in interlocking scrolls on the thorax at the base of the black, button head. The antennae, as the sunlight struck them, sheened in an iridescense, predominantly purple.

"Magnificent." I breathed, bending close to the jar.

He was pleased.

"Look closely. She is the culmination of twenty years' work. Twenty years. . . cross-breeding. . .inter-breeding. . .failure. Only two of the final eggs hatched into larvae, only two. Only one of the chrysalises matured." He shook his head. His voice carried an overtone of sadness.

"Examine it closely. The *Kreutch lepidopteron*. Notice, I use the singular. The first and last of its species. Perfection, gentlemen. In a manner of speaking this solitary butterfly is the best of me. It has become my soul."

He reached up and began to unscrew the ventilated top of the ordinary two-quart jar.

We stared, fascinated into silence.

Then, very deliberately, he removed the cap and spilled the butterfly out the window into the fresh April air.

We watched, the three of us, as the gorgeous creature beat its wings and climbed higher. . . higher. . . melting at last into the April sky, vanishing.

Dr. Kreutch remained at the window gazing upward long after the butterfly had disappeared. Then he closed the window, drew the shade, and carried the empty jar back to his desk, handling it as fondly as though it still kept his butterfly.

After replacing the jar, he turned to us, removed his spectacles and began polishing them with his handkerchief, as he talked.

"Now to business. The disappearance of my wife has come to your attention. Very well. You will remember I told you only one of the two chrysalises reached the imaginal stage—matured? My wife was a lovely woman and our affection was genuine. But at times she lost patience with my—ah—preoccupation.

"One evening she became highly emotional. I found her in this room puncturing the other chrysalis of my *Kreutch lepidopteron*—goring it with a brooch pin. And she was reaching for the second one, when I took her throat in my hands.

"In my garden is a rare and extraordinarily beautiful Rosewood tree. Come, gentlemen, I shall show you her grave."

The blood pulsed powerfully in my head. I heard myself trying to shout, "Dr. Kreutch."

Dave's fingers closed painfully on my arm. The words dissolved in my throat. Dave's voice was almost calm.

"Certainly, Dr. Kreutch. Please show us where she is."

* * *

Two hours later, Dave and I stood once more outside the ivy-covered gate. I looked at him. The lines in his face were deeper. Horror pulled at the corners of his mouth.

"Good Lord!" I said. "Our papers send us for a story of some strange new butterfly, and—good Lord!"

"Yes," said Dave. "The poor devil thought we were the police." Then Dave tried to smile. "He was wrong about his Krait, too. When I went back into the house, I found him sitting in that room, with the snake in his hands. He figured it would take two and a half minutes. It was another twenty seconds, at least, before he died."

The Secret of Glamis Castle

Gloomy Glamis Castle in Scotland, the oldest inhabited house in Britain, seat of the Earls of Strathmore, traditional scene of the murder of Duncan by Macbeth, home of the present Queen of England — is also the guardian, within its 15 foot walls, of a dreadful secret that has been kept inviolate for hundreds of years.

The mystery of Glamis revolves about a walled-up chamber, whose location and terrible secret are known to only three persons at one time: the Earl of Strathmore, his eldest son (or next heir), and the steward of the estate.

This secret is always revealed to the eldest son on the night of his 21st birthday. This is done, according to rumour, by the three of them tearing down the masonry wall that conceals the mystery, after which it is immediately rebuilt, not to be opened for another generation.

Many have sought an answer to this uncanny enigma -- Sir Augustus Rumbold, Sir Walter Scott, Lord Playfair and Augustus Hare, to mention only a few.

ONCE AN INGENIOUS ATTEMPT WAS MADE TO DISCOVER THE ROOM DURING THE ABSENCE OF ONE OF THE FORMER EARLS. A PARTY OF GUESTS, LED BY THE COUNTESS, HUNG TOWELS OUT OF EVERY CASEMENT ON THE SUPPOSITION THAT THE ROOM MUST HAVE A WINDOW, CONCLUDING THAT THE WINDOW NOT SHOWING A TOWEL WOULD BE IT. THIS, LIKE ALL OTHER ATTEMPTS, FAILED.

THROUGH THE CENTURIES MANY THEORIES HAVE BEEN EVOLVED AS TO WHAT THE TERRIBLE SECRET MAY BE. THESE MAY BE READ IN ANY HISTORY OF GLAMIS CASTLE. THE MOST POPULAR NOTION, TO THOSE EAGER TO MAKE THE MOST OF IT, IS THAT A HIDEOUS MONSTER OF FABULOUS AGE, LURKS IN THIS DUNGEON.

WHATEVER THE SECRET MAY BE, NO HEIR TO THE MYSTERY HAS EVER TOLD, ALTHOUGH SOME, WITH THE SKEPTICISM OF YOUTH AND BEFORE THEY HAD VISITED THE FORBIDDING DUNGEON, HAVE PROMISED TO DO SO.

CLAUDE GEORGE BOWES-LYON PRESENT EARL OF STRATHMORE FATHER OF QUEEN ELIZABETH

THE EARL OF STRATHMORE WHO DIED IN 1905, SAID TO AN INQUIRER, "IF YOU COULD GUESS THE NATURE OF THIS SECRET, YOU WOULD GO DOWN ON YOUR KNEES AND THANK GOD IT IS NOT YOURS."

••• ◆ Homicidal

Dramatic Novelette of a Macabre Triangle

By Bruno Fischer

Luscious Della was a warm-blooded girl whose scarecrow husband— figuring she was two-timing with me—bought a knife ... and brooded on classical slaughter.

CHAPTER ONE

Tuesday, 3 P.M.

And suddenly her husband was in the hall. . . .

LEAL FLOYD tested the sharpness of the six-inch blade with the ball of his thumb. "Murder," he said, "is justified only when the reason for it is as profound as the deed."

We lounged in the shade of the barn. Wearing only shorts and sneakers, Leal sat on the ground with his legs crossed like a skinny Buddha, contemplating his hunting knife.

"How much would be enough motive?" I drawled, suppressing a yawn. "A million dollars? Or would a mere fifty grand do?"

Leal snorted as he gently ran the blade over an oil stone. "Material gain is shabby motive for the most dramatic act of which man is capable—that of taking another's life. The noblest killers of literature murdered because of pride or self-respect. Hamlet killed for revenge, Othello smothered his wife out of jealousy."

The discussion didn't particularly in-terest me, though I'd started it. I had come upon him sharpening the knife and had mentioned casually that it could be a deadly weapon. And he had started talking rather gloomily of murder.

I stood up. "What do you want it for?" I asked him suddenly.

"Want what?"

"That hunting knife? You don't hunt."

Homestead ... ◆ ◆ ◆

He lifted his eyes. They were black, deep-set, somber—a poet's eyes. "I scarcely know," he said. "I saw it in town yesterday. It fascinated me and I bought it."

"Didn't it come sharpened from the store?"

"I suppose so." He pulled one of the curly black hairs out of his thin, bare chest and waved the blade at it. The hair parted neatly.

I found myself shivering slightly in spite of the heat.

"Have to get to work," I said and sauntered to the house.

Della Floyd was drying dishes in the big, old-fashioned kitchen. Being a woman, she wore one more garment than her husband—a skimpy flowered halter. Between Della and Leal, I felt somewhat overdressed in white ducks and polo shirt.

She couldn't be called beautiful, though she had a figure that inevitably drew the male gaze. Her smile was warm and cozy, making almost every man feel that she liked him, without giving him exaggerated ideas about how much she liked him. And she had a verve and buoyancy that always made it pleasant to be in her company.

"How about going swimming, Harry?" she asked me.

"I've got to work," I said.

She threw down the dishtowel. "Leal is such a poor swimmer that he doesn't care for it, and I hate to go alone."

"Maybe later, Della," I said.

She grabbed my arm with both hands. "Come on, Harry," she pleaded, hugging my arm to her.

Those friendly physical gestures had no intimate significance. I was a friend of the family—a man to be kissed hello and good-by in public, in front of her husband, and to have his arm hugged on occasion. Nothing more.

All the same, a man can't be completely objective about an attractive, inadequately clad woman clinging to his arm. I felt somewhat uneasy as her soft voice persisted: "It's too hot to shut yourself in your room, Harry."

Through the open kitchen door I saw Leal approach the house. Sunlight glistened on sweat beading like dew the curly black hair on his skinny chest. The hunting knife dangled from his right hand.

I pulled away from Della, mumbling, "I'm way behind on the book." I left the kitchen before Leal came in.

Thirty minutes later I had writen just two sentences. So I sat at the window looking over Leal Floyd's farm. It was a typical New England farm, and, typically, no longer farmed.

Because Leal Floyd's great grandfather had established a successful shoe industry near Boston, Leal could afford to indulge his whims. One was writing poetry which nobody bought or read. Another was passing up all the aristocratic Boston girls who hankered for him—and his money—and marrying a New York waitress. Still another was buying this farm last spring and dragging me, who was a friend as well as an architect, here to remodel the place.

At that time I had been writing a book on small houses, but Leal had pointed out that I could do his plans and write the book at the same time.

So here I was after a week, and my book just about where it had been when I arrived—and not a line of the plans drawn.

I couldn't get myself set. Maybe it was just a plain case of midsummer listlessness. Instead of working, I kept wondering why on earth Leal had bought that knife.

Tuesday, 5:15 P.M.

I WAS still sitting at the window when Della came out of the house. She had changed into two strips of white cloth which current convention decreed was proper attire for a woman only if she appeared in it in public close to a swimming place. I liked the way her hips undulated as she walked toward the pond. With my arms on the ledge, I leaned out of the window to watch her.

Gradually I became aware of somebody else down there. He was so long and thin and motionless that he might have been part of the vegetation. He was staring fixedly up at me—watching me look after his wife.

Hastily I withdrew my head. A moment later I was angry at myself for acting as if I'd done something wrong. I turned back to paper and pen.

It was no good. After a while I gave up

trying. I got into my swimming trunks and went downstairs.

I was passing the barn when Leal appeared around the corner of it. He was absently whittling on a piece of wood with his new hunting knife.

"Going swimming?" he asked.

"Thought I'd take a dip."

"I'll go with you."

I offered to wait there for him while he got his trunks, but he shook his head. "I don't feel like swimming," he said. "I'll just go along."

We walked the thousand remaining feet to the pond without saying a word to each other. All the time he kept whittling on that piece of wood.

There was a small swimming dock and a float about a hundred feet out. Della was lying on the float, under the glaring sun a contrast of much tanned skin and a lot less white bathing suit. I kicked my shoes off and dove. I swam to the float.

As I climbed up the ladder, Della turned on her side to me and gave me her smile. I twisted my head. Leal was sitting on the dock, on his legs like a skinny Buddha, and the sun glistened on the bright keen blade of the knife with which he whittled pointlessly.

Wednesday, 11:40 A.M.

SOMETHING had come over Leal Floyd. He'd become quieter than usual. I sensed a charged brooding in him, as before a storm.

Leal can afford a dozen servants if he wants them, but he hasn't even one on the farm. He says that he can't feel free and unrestrained with servants around. The result is that Della has to do all the housework and cooking, but she doesn't seem to mind. She has too much buoyancy to let work bother her.

At breakfast this morning she asked me to drive her into town for shopping. About the only accomplishment she lacks is the confidence and ability to drive a car.

"I'll drive you," Leal said quickly.

"But yesterday Harry said there were some things he wanted to buy in town," Della said. "It isn't necessary for both of you to go."

I recalled that yesterday at lunch I'd mentioned that I had to do a bit of personal shopping. It wasn't important. I should have stayed to work. But as Leal didn't say any more about it. I supposed that he preferred me to go, and it was the least I could do in return for his hospitality.

So I drove Della into town, and it was lots of fun being with her. She was good company. She did her shopping and I did mine, and then we had ice-cream sodas. We were walking from the ice cream parlor to the parked car when I saw Leal.

It was on the main street, and heat was rising in waves from the baked sidewalks and road, and for a moment he looked like a shimmering mirage standing across the street in a drugstore doorway. But there was nobody quite as tall or gaunt, and nobody else had as garish a Basque shirt as the one he was wearing. He was watching us.

I became aware that Della's hand was through my arm, that she held it tightly, that the way we walked and talked made us look like lovers on a spree. I opened my mouth to tell her that her husband was across the street, but I didn't. And neither did I let on to Leal that I had seen him. I walked on with Della to the car.

Leal has two cars on the farm—the sedan we'd taken and a jeep. He had followed us in the jeep, and he beat us back to the farm by taking back roads. I knew because the jeep was in the driveway when we got back. And when Della and I got out of the sedan, I saw a shadow in one of the downstairs windows, a faint stirring.

I got a little nervous when Della, turning suddenly, ran a soft, hot hand over my cheek. "You're a darling for driving me in, Harry," she cooed, and gave my cheek another pat.

I wish she wouldn't do such things—especially when her husband is watching.

CHAPTER TWO

Wednesday, 10:30 P.M.

NOW I know that Leal— But wait. Let me put it down the way it happened and then look at it and try to retain a sense of proportion. I wouldn't be the first man who'd let imagination run away with him.

Our meals used to be sprightly, but at supper this evening Della had to handle the conversation practically alone. Lunch had been the same way. Leal's fault. The last couple of days he'd got moody, and I caught it from him.

"What's come over you men?" Della demanded when we reached dessert and coffee. "You're acting like your best friend just died."

"As if," Leal corrected. "I've told you time and again that like isn't a conjunction."

Della said tartly: "You should've known when you married a waitress that her grammar wouldn't be perfect."

That was the first time I'd ever known Della to show annoyance. Maybe the general mood was contagious.

Leal didn't bother to reply.

I stood up. I wanted to get away from both of them—from Leal who'd got a cockeyed notion into his head about his wife and me; from Della who was too obtrusively exciting in shorts and halter, into which she had changed shortly after we had returned from town. I said: "I think I'll do a sketch of the barn."

"I didn't know you were an artist too," Della said, turning a smile on for me. Her high spirits couldn't be downed for more than a minute at a time.

"An architect's sketch of what the barn will look like when it's remodeled," I explained.

I went up to my room and fetched a pad and drafting set, then I set a chair halfway between the house and barn and started the sketch. Leal wanted the barn converted into a recreation building, at the same time retaining the structure's basic appearance. I thought the idea rather corny, but he was paying the bill.

"How's it going?" Della asked.

She had come up from the house and was standing beside me, looking down at the pad on my knees.

"Okay," I said, hoping that she wouldn't pat my cheek or lean against me or anything like that.

She didn't. She walked on toward the barn. I forced myself to concentrate on the sketch instead of the sway of her hips. I started to sketch in the roof and then suddenly wondered if the ancient beams would be strong enough to hold up the roof when the support of the hayloft was removed. I put down the pad and went to the barn.

Della was in there. A few days ago her cocker spaniel had had three puppies in one of the stalls. Della was playing with them while the mother growled anxiously.

Della glanced up at me over a bare shoulder. "Aren't they adorable, Harry?"

I agreed that the puppies were adorable and examined the twelve-inch solid oak crossbeams. They had been put in a hundred years ago and looked as if they would last another hundred. I left the barn and started back to my sketch pad.

Leal was coming toward the barn. He walked with his head down, his narrow shoulders hunched—not rapidly, but something terrifically urgent in his long-legged stride. The naked hunting knife was in his hand.

When he saw me, he stopped. I stopped. He looked at me and I looked at the knife.

Good God, I thought, *he's going to kill me!*

It couldn't have been more than a couple of seconds that we stood facing each other, but hours had never seemed so long. Then he bent and picked up a twig and started to whittle it. His bony hand shook.

"I had a look at the barn timbers," I heard myself say. "They're still pretty strong."

Leal nodded abstractedly. There was practically nothing left of the twig, but he continued to slice at it.

I moved on to my chair. I picked up the sketch pad and a pencil, but I didn't draw another line.

My mind went back over the last few minutes. Della had come out of the house and said a few words to me and then had gone on to the barn. Very shortly after that I had followed her. And Leal, watching us as he had watched us for the last two days, had added that up to mean that we had arranged to meet in the barn. To make love, he'd thought, and he had grabbed up the knife and had gone after me.

Then my sudden reappearance had startled him, bewildered him. According to the crazy pattern his jealousy had evolved, I was supposed to be holding Della in my arms. If I had stayed in the barn a little longer, if he had come in on Della snuggling up to me as she so often did. . . .

I found myself shivering in the heat. Abruptly my head came up. Where was Leal now? I hadn't seen or heard him since I had retuned to the chair. Maybe he had slipped up behind me. He and his knife.

I whirled so quickly that I almost fell out of the chair. Leal was nowhere in sight. But Della was coming from the barn. The sinking sun caught her honey-colored hair, and as she moved toward me her walk was all feminine.

I snatched up my drafting paraphernalia and went into the house and up-stairs. I wanted no part of her at all.

In my room, I wondered if the whole thing was just my imagination. Leal was my friend. Perhaps was forcing upon myself the belief that he was out to kill me.

I scribbled the following list:

Item: he is spying on Della and me at every opportunity, and in particular he followed us to town this morning.

Item: for the last few days he has been unnaturally moody and indrawn.

Item: he bought a deadly knife for which he has no apparent use.

Item: yesterday beside the barn he justified murder under certain circumstances.

Item: he followed me to the barn this evening, when he thought I had gone there to make love to Della, and the knife was in his hand.

I read over this list. It could have meant nothing—or everything.

Then I heard Della and Leal coming up the stairs—but not together. First Della and then Leal. She went directly to her room, he to his.

It was too early to go to bed. I guess they'd had nothing else to do. Neither had I.

But before I went into bed, I'd make sure to lock the door.

Thursday, 2 A.M.

SOME time during the night I awoke covered with sweat. It was as if even in sleep I had been listening to something, and now, fully awake, I heard it—a sound not louder than the thumping of my heart. Moonlight flowed in through the window, and by it I saw the doorknob turn.

Killing a fellow human being is sometimes essential to one's pride and self-respect. That was what he had said yesterday afternoon as he had sharpened his knife.

The doorknob stopped turning. He had assured himself that the door was locked. There was a soft rap. "Harry," Leal whispered in the hall.

I could imagine him standing out there, tall and gaunt in pajamas, and the razor-sharp knife held along his thigh. The locked door had defeated his purpose. Now he was trying to get at me through subtle means.

"Harry," he called again, so low that Della, in her room, would not hear.

I lay flat on my back without breathing.

I did not hear him move away, did not hear his bare feet on the hall floor, but I heard his own door open and close.

In the morning I was getting the hell out of this house.

Thursday, 11 A.M.

At breakfast I announced that I had to return to the city at once. And I watched Leal.

Across the table his eyes met mine, and I thought I detected mockery in their somber depths. "You've hardly started on the work you came here to do," he said.

"Something came up," I said. "I'll be back in a couple of days."

"Can't you attend to it by phone, Harry?" he argued.

This was another item in the balance sheet of evidence. Believing that I was having an affair with his wife, he should be anxious to get me out of his house. Instead, he wanted me to stay. To be available for his knife.

"A client needs my personal attention," I insisted.

Then Della spoke up brightly. "I've been planning to go to New York for a few days. I'm anxious to visit my sister and shop in the Fifth Avenue stores. Suppose I drive you to New York, Harry, and Saturday or Sunday you'll drive back with me."

I could have slapped her. Leal would be dead certain that we had arranged this meeting in advance to get together.

I waited for him to refuse to let her go. But he just looked at her, then without comment finished his coffee and left the table.

"I'll be ready in an hour, Harry," Della told me, giving my shoulder a pat.

At that, I thought, I would get away from the house, which was all I wanted. She would chauffeur me to New York, and that would probably be the last I'd see of her and Leal. I went upstairs to pack.

I was snapping the lock on my bag when downstairs Della screamed. I started for the door, hesitated. Leal would have his knife, and I was unarmed.

Through the floor I heard Della groan. I ran my tongue over my lips, called myself a coward, plunged down the stairs.

They were in the kitchen. Della sat on the floor, rocking from side to side and clinging with both hands to her right foot. Leal knelt at her side.

"What happened?" I asked.

Leal turned his head to me. "I'm a clumsy idiot," he said tonelessly. "I was carrying a bottle of milk to the refrigerator and dropped it on Della's foot."

The bottle lay unbroken on its side. It hadn't been opened and the cap was still tightly on.

He had deliberately dropped the bottle on her foot to keep her from going with me.

"Let's look at your foot," I said.

Della took her hands away. She was still in housecoat and slippers, and the bottle had fallen on her bare instep. There was a bruise, but nothing seemed broken.

"We'll soak the foot," I said, "and then—"

"I'll attend to that," Leal burst out savagely. As if reminding me that he was, after all, her husband. "I thought you were in a hurry to leave for New York." One corner of his mouth lifted sardonically. "I'm afraid Della won't be able to drive you in to New York now, Harry."

I stood up. "I'll call a taxi."

"That won't be neecssary," Leal said. "I'll drive you to the station."

Now he seemed anxious for me to go.

He reached down a hand to help Della up to her feet. When she rose and leaned against him for support, I saw something in his eyes that frightened me more than anything else that had happened in the last two days.

I knew that I couldn't leave her here alone with him—and his knife.

I took out my handkerchief to wipe sweat from my face. It was real enough sweat. "Today will be another scorcher," I said. "I hate to think of what it will be like in New York."

"Then why go?" Della said it quickly, urgently, and I wondered if she too had guessed and was afraid to be alone with him.

Leal said nothing.

"I guess I really don't have to," I said. "After all, I'm supposed to be working for you, Leal."

He turned expressionless eyes to me. I squirmed. I felt as if I'd just admitted my guilt. He had it down pat in his thoughts. I'd been ready to leave with Della, but when she was prevented from going because of her hurt foot, I changed my mind. Conclusive enough evidence to a jealousy-inflamed brain.

But what could I do? Della was no more to me than the wife of a friend—or of a man who had been my friend—but I couldn't walk out on her and leave her to the mercy of his knife.

I went to my room. Della was soaking her foot in the living room, and Leal was with her.

Maybe I had my impressions crossed and all along she'd been his intended victim. Or both of us. Then at breakfast something had happened to concentrate his murderous jealousy on his wife, instead of her supposed lover. Her offer to drive me to New York and stay there as long as I did must have seemed to him an intolerable flaunting of her supposed unfaithfulness.

Pride and self-respect justifying murder. And when he had said that outside the barn two days ago, he had called Shakespeare's Othello—who had smothered his wife because he believed her unfaithful—a noble character.

So then Leal had wanted me out of the house so that he could attend to Della in his own way and time.

They were very quiet in the living room. My door was open and I could hear every sound down there. They had not exchanged a word in a long time.

Thursday, 10:20 P.M.

All the next day Leal whittled a boat with his hunting knife. Della, her foot bandaged, lay on the couch reading a novel. I sat at the table and worked on the house plans. What I designed wasn't important; I was just occupying my hands and giving myself an excuse for staying in that room. Leal, hunched in a chair, whittled into the fireplace.

He had the knife and I had only my hands. Still, I think I could take him if I remained alert. I'm three inches shorter, but forty pounds heavier.

Possibly I could persuade Della to leave this house. I'd have to sneak up behind him and knock him out. Then what? Then he'd go after us—maybe not right away, maybe taking his time so that we'd never know where and when the blow would fall.

Better to wait for it right here. But waiting isn't easy.

That night before I went to bed I got a hatchet from the tool shed. It's at least as effective a weapon as a knife.

Della went to her room at eight o'clock. Leal carried her up the stairs. I hovered about until he left her room, which was almost as soon as he placed her on her bed. Then he went to his own room.

Tonight I decided not to lock my door. I wouldn't go to bed. I'd sit in the darkness with the hatchet near my hand.

CHAPTER THREE

Friday, 1 A.M.

SOFTLY a door opened and closed. I heard the sound only because I was listening for it. I'd left my own door open a couple of inches. At the far end of the hall there was a small window which admitted enough moonlight to reveal a shadow crossing the hall.

My hand sweated on the hatchet.

The shadow didn't come toward my room. For a long moment it hesitated in the center of the hall, then swung quickly, as if in sudden determination, and headed toward Della's room. The door opened, and beyond it there was light—and in a hand I saw a hunting knife.

I leaped out of my room. An instant after I moved, the shadow became fully revealed. It wasn't tall and gaunt. It was an attractive woman in clinging blue pajamas.

Della heard me and turned. I had barely time to duck the hatchet out of sight behind my back. Then I just stood there. Now I was a shadow.

"Harry?" she whispered.

"Yes." A I moved toward her, I pushed the hatchet down the back of my pants. My belt held it.

I looked down at the knife in her hand, Leal's hunting knife.

She gave a nervous little laugh. "I stole it from him. I took it from his room just now. It was driving me mad."

"The knife?" I asked rather stupidly.

"Harry, I'm afraid of him." Her hand lay flat on my chest. "Do you know that he deliberately dropped that milk bottle on my foot?"

"I know."

Della was close against me. There was nothing intimate in that; merely a frightened woman clinging to a man she could trust.

"I don't know what's come over him these last few days," she said. "Sometimes I think—"

And suddenly her husband was in the hall . . . a gaunt, motionless shape in flappy pajamas. Light from his room across the hall flowed out to meet the patch of light in which we stood in front of Della's room.

She didn't spring guiltily away from me. That wasn't her way. She merely put an inch of distance between us.

"I thought my foot was better," she said calmly to her husband, "but when I came out of my room I fell and Harry heard me cry out. He came out and picked me up."

It wasn't a good lie, but no lie would have been convincing. As a matter of fact, what Leal believed was another lie—that he had caught us in an embrace. There was something sad in his face as he looked at us. I was glad that he didn't have the knife.

I had the hunting knife now. Della had slipped it into my pants pocket so that Leal wouldn't see that she had it.

"Are you all right now, Della?" Leal asked woodenly.

"Do you mind helping me into bed, darling?" she said.

Leal crossed the hall and lifted her and carried her into her room. I stood in the hall, watching them through the open door, until he came out. He closed her door.

"She's no good, Harry," he said. "She'll be no better for you than she is for me."

"What the hell are you talking about?" I said.

He ran his tongue over his lower lip. Then he said, "Good night," and went rigidly and hurriedly into his room.

Back in my own room, I took the hatchet out of my pants and the knife out of my pocket. I sat down to wait out the night.

Friday, 2 P.M.

Again, as yesterday, I told them at breakfast that I had to return to New York. "I'm not getting any work done here," I said. "I may as well attend to my New York client."

Della was pouring my coffee. Her foot had got a lot better overnight; she limped, but she could move about. The coffee pot paused over my cup, and it was as if my words had washed her face of expression.

"Must you?" she asked quietly.

"I'll be back in a few days," I said.

As she moved away from my side of the table, I noticed the unnatural slump of her shoulders.

Leal only said: "I'll drive you to the station, Harry, as soon as you're ready."

I was ready in twenty minutes. As I came down the stairs, I heard Leal ask Della if she had seen his hunting knife.

"I'm sure I left it down here on the mantle," he said.

"You're always mislaying your things," Della said.

Fingering the hunting knife in my pocket, I descended the rest of the stairs. "I'm ready, Leal," I said.

Della didn't come along. She waved good-by to me from the door. On the way, there wasn't a thing Leal and I had to say to each other. When I got out of the car at the station, we muttered good-by without shaking hands.

I gave Leal's sedan a five-minute start and then got into a taxi. On the highway, some half-mile from the house, I paid off the driver. There was a driveway, but I took an overgrown footpath through brush. I transferred Leal's knife from my pocket to my belt.

The house was very quiet. I knew that Leal had returned because I saw the sedan. I stood behind a Dutch elm and sweated in the city clothes I'd put on to go to New York. It was another sweltering day.

After a while I wondered what good I could do behind that tree. Whatever happened, wouldn't happen here out in the open. Or maybe it had happened already. I was trying to decide how I could get across the clearing and sneak into the house without being seen when Leal appeared.

He came out of the back door, and he wore swimming trunks. But where was Della? The day was hot enough to induce even Leal to go for a swim, but wouldn't Della also go?

Unless she couldn't. . . .

Then I heard her call gayly from the pond, "Leal?"

He replied, "Coming, Della." He disappeared into the apple orchard between the house and pond.

Sweating in my city clothes, I followed. The last of the apple trees was a hundred feet from the pond. I stood behind it, and my right hand was on the knife in my belt.

Della was standing on the float in the bright sunlight. She was a rich brown except where the two white strips of cloth covered it. "Come in, darling," she called to her husband. "The water's fine."

Leal didn't know how to dive. He climbed down the ladder and thrust himself toward the float with wildly flailing arms and legs. He could just about make that hundred feet.

Della dove cleanly off the dock and swam to meet him. When she reached him, she put her hands on his shoulders and lifted herself out of the water up to her hips. Leal's head disappeared.

It took me a couple of seconds to get it. Then I ran, shedding my jacket and shirt on the way. When I reached the edge of the dock, Leal's head reappeared for an instant. Della leaped out of the water, seemed to fall on him.

I pulled off my shoes and dove. They were only fifty feet away. I came up within a foot of Della, and then suddenly for the first time she knew that I wasn't on the train to New York.

I struck her with my open hand.

FOR the next minute I was too busy with Leal to pay attention to her. He fought me as I brought him up, but when he saw that I wasn't Della he relaxed and let me tow him in. He had just enough strength left to climb the ladder to the dock. Then he flopped down on his face.

I looked back. Della was swimming leasurely toward the dock. She came dripping up the ladder and shook out her loose wet hair and turned a smile on me.

"It's a good thing you were here, Harry," she said sweetly. "I couldn't have got him out by myself."

Leal turned on his side, facing us. "You tried to drown me, Della." He said that without hate—just unutterable weariness.

"How ridiculous, darling," she said.

The knife was still in my belt. I looked down at it and then at her. "And I thought all along that it was Leal who was set on murder. That he was out to kill me or you or both of us. And I came back to protect you from him. Go on, keep smiling, Della. It's a good laugh."

She wasn't smiling now. She crossed her arms on her chest, as if the air had turned cold. "You—you saw?"

"Plenty," I said. "Leal and I both know you tried to drown him. I suppose last night you got his knife from downstairs to murder him. Maybe your idea was to frame me for it, but I broke it up when I came into the hall. And besides, this way was safer all around. Nobody would have been able to prove that he hadn't drowned by accident."

She tossed her hair. "You can't prove anything, anyway."

"Maybe not," I conceded. "I suppose it was Leal's money you wanted."

"I hate him!" she burst out with a fury that shook her. "I hated him when he asked me to marry him. All he had was money. I thought I could stand him—but I couldn't. I wanted to be free."

"Free with his money," I said dryly, "which you would inherit on his death."

She stared at me open-mouthed, then swung away and ran off the dock. Her limp was all gone. I started after her.

"Let her go," Leal said quietly.

He was sitting up with his head in his hands.

"I'm sorry, Leal," I said. "I had an idea that you—"

"That I intended to kill you?" He nodded slowly. "I heard you tell Della. Because I was spying on you and her, Harry? I admit it. You see, I suspected what she was. I didn't trust her. But I wanted to be sure before I kicked her out of my house. In fact, the other night I went to your room to talk it over with you, man to man, but your door was locked."

While I lay breathless in bed, sure that he had come to murder me. But why couldn't he have talked it over later?

I said: "Several days ago you justified murder under certain circumstances—circumstances like this."

His mouth twisted. "Words, Harry. You should know by now that a poet makes a game of words. A literary game."

"But this knife," I persisted, taking it out of my belt.

"I've always liked knives. That's the small boy in me. It meant nothing."

I thought: Didn't it? But I had no answer. I'll never have.

He bought that knife because he liked to whittle with a six-inch hunting knife. Maybe.

THE END

DEATH IS A DAME

(Continued from page 27)

this, Foss. You were infatuated with Zelda and madly jealous of her. That's why you killed Squire, then shot Zelda, too, in that penthouse, and made her death look like a suicide.

"But since then it's been preying on your conscience — particularly because your wife is such a sweet, unsuspecting little girl. It reached the point where it wouldn't let you sleep—you couldn't stand it any more. So then, overwhelmed with remorse, you shot yourself."

He was smiling pungently. "With an empty gun?"

Her face a mask of stony cruelty, she moved quickly closer to him, pushing the gun out at arm's length—pushing it upward in a dead aim at the center of his forehead. She pulled the trigger—once, then again—and heard only empty-sounding clicks.

"Damn you!" She screamed it and in a burst of fury, throwing the useless gun aside, flung herself at him.

For an instant he knew the helpless panic of the trapped. He was poised on the chair, with nothing behind him except a window — a window looking out on space, with a narrow, low-railed balcony outside it—and an enraged woman hurling herself at him. For another instant he could imagine people reading of his death in the papers — *Accidental Plunge from 10th Story Window* — could hear them commenting idly, "Guess even a professional dancer loses his balance once in a while."

Then all his supple muscles snapped at once in a desperate, instinctive effort to evade the girl's murderous thrust.

He leaped, projecting himself out of the corner, forming himself into a hurtling ball in midair, spinning over the girl's deadly arms. He bounded toward the center of the room—and as he alighted on his toes he heard the crash of glass, and

SHOCK

a ragged, hoarse scream of doom—an ugly sound that never could have torn itself from the sweet throat of Anne.

He spun about. She was gone. The window was vacant, framed with broken teeth of glass, shards glittering on the floor under it. Again he heard the ugly scream, this time from far below—a horrible sound suddenly ended.

Foss Dayne went slowly to the window, leaned out and gazed at the street far down. There were two figures moving across from a doorway. The man, Dayne knew, was Sergeant Kirk; he had been on watch. The other, he knew even more surely, was Joyce—Joyce the dark, the bold, the lovely, pausing now to lift her face to him. . . .

They were bending over a small dark spot on the pavement—all that was left of Zelda—the period on a dark and evil life.

THE END

(Continued from page 31)

presser had slammed the door right in her face! Slowly and ponderously she put into motion the machinery that would get her to her feet. Poisonous hatred gleamed in her little pig eyes.

HERMAN finished his supper and was washing the few dishes, when he heard a noise in the street that sounded like an auto crash. He walked into the front room and saw Rosie leaning out the window. She turned her head as he entered.

"So we don't talk about Myron?" she cried. "My boy Myron, by my first marriage, who watched you workin' on that hunk of wood and went off to the Navy. He ain't never comin' back now, so you don't need to work on that lousy hunk of wood no more." She began to laugh. "Take a look. It's down there, down there in the street—what's left of it." She laughed until every layer of fat was undulating, flowing, rolling.

Herman stared at her, then went into the bedroom. The work table was empty. He searched the bedroom carefully; he examined the living room, and opened the door to the hall.

"Down there I tell you!" His wife was laughing until the tears rolled from her eyes. "Down there, in the street!"

The newspapers said later Herman went temporarily nuts. He didn't. He simply pushed Rosie through the window. It took him a long time. He had to gather the fat and stuff it through the frame. Rosie was not laughing now. She was screaming at the top of her lungs. The hotel across the street became a blaze of lights as people watched Herman push his wife through the window. Passersby on the street looked up, curious, horrified, silent.

She was half-way out, her arms and legs flailing the air like a huge beetle turned upon its back. Herman placed his shoulders against her bulk and shoved with all his might. Rosie's screaming rose to a high crescendo. It reached the pitch of high C as she suddenly shot out of the window, like a gigantic, ripe fruit being pared from its skin. The crescendo of her screaming curved downward with her body and died suddenly as she hit the street.

She fell in the street, a great barrel of lard, her blood splattering into the lobby of the hotel. It was all of Rosie Willis that ever managed to reach the hotel of her dreams.

When the police cars arrived, they found Herman down on his knees in the street, carefully picking up the pieces of his little ship.

(Continued from page 37)

You could have gotten that dope out of the papers, you know."

"But the fact that Michael Burns and Miss Dikes moved out that same night I was shot—!"

Lieutenant Weber scratched gently over his right ear. More scurf fell on his dark coat. "I figure it this way, Brayton. You and Burns were both after the girl. Burns won. They were scared of you. You acted funny. They took off and you rigged up a story of shooting yourself in the arm and then tossed your gun in the drink. Your idea was revenge. You built your idea on the fact that one of her dates fell in front of a train. That's all you've got for us."

I stood up. "Look, Lieutenant. I didn't dream this up, you know."

He smiled tiredly. "You better relax, fella. Psycho, weren't you?"

Suddenly I understood. I leaned on the desk. "No, I was not a psycho. I flew sixty-one missions and was shipped back to the states on account of combat fatigue. Then the war ended."

"You better take it easy, Brayton."

I turned and walked out. . . .

But I know one thing. Burns hasn't showed up at his job since that night. And she had a gun when she left the bench. They lived a block and a half from the river. When the tide is right, a body will go on out to sea.

I feel as if I should do something to stop her. I don't know where she is. I think she's still in town. Once I thought I saw her, but I lost her in the crowd. I spend a lot of my time where the crowds are thickest. That's where she'll be.

Keep your eyes open. She's a lean-flanked lovely girl with vague gray eyes and thick black hair. Her face sometimes has a pinched, white look, but her lips are warm and heavy. She probably uses another name now. I think she knows I'm looking for her.